HER OBSIDIAN BOW

A GUARDIANS OF CAMELOT PORTAL FANTASY NOVEL

SARAH BIGLOW

For information contact; www.sarah-biglow.com

Edited by: Alecia Goodman, Under Wraps Publishing Services

Cover Design by: Deranged Doctor Design

Interior Art by: Therena Carlin

ISBN: 978-1-955988-70-4

Published by Sarah Biglow March 2026

10 9 8 7 6 5 4 3 2 1

 Formatted with Vellum

FROM THE AUTHOR

Special Thanks to:

Victoria Psomiadis, Ryan Scott James, Brian Grimes, Anonymous Reader, maileguy, Rosie Pease, Samantha Newberry, Tanya Young, Heiko Koenig, Yara Dijkstra, Samantha Ghormley, GhostCat, pjk, Jackie Kripas, Elizabeth W., Ayl, Matthew Walker, Chris Clayton, Francesco Tehrani, Stacy Ward, Catherine McP., Mono, Emily Welsby, Sue Frecker, Diane Hansebout, Lavar, Anna McCluskey, Vicki Hsu, Molly Zenk, Lorenzo, Michael W. Kerr, Scott Casey, Kathryn, Bonniejean Boettecher, Katherine Malloy, Melissa Showers, Gerald P. McDaniel, Finley Ymir, Niels Starfari, Stephen Ballentine, StarbuckApolloFemshepKaidanAliCole,, Danae, Susanna, PippiMD, Isaac Dansicker, Steven Byrd, Robin Hill, John Idlor, Nicola Thompson, Stacy Shuda, Adam Brooks, Courtney Arnold, Margaret St. John, Molly J. Stanton, Cathy McLoughlin, Billye Herndon, Justise Briones, Amanda, Alexandra Corrsin, Maria Mejia, Josefine Bällsten, Vanessa Goodwin, Jade Feinics, and Karen Bulgarelli.

CHAPTER
ONE

A thin coating of snow covered the ground outside the cabin as early morning sunlight filtered through the window. I was warm beneath the blankets as I took in the peaceful silence of the space around me. It had been nearly a month since the ordeal with the Syndicate and finally it felt like I could breathe again. I rolled over to find Taron snoring softly beside me, one arm thrown over his head. I snuggled up against his torso, soaking in the constant warmth he gave off. I could almost envision myself staying in bed indefinitely at his side.

The lack of constant danger was good for us. So far, it was casual and the intensity I'd witnessed in Dublin had receded. I could indulge in this togetherness without the expectation of labeling things.

For now, we were keeping it to ourselves. Our secret early morning rendezvous had shifted from the lake to the cabin thanks to the weather and that had been the push we needed to take things to the next level. My fingers trailed along his cheek, and he gave a soft sigh before opening one eye.

I leaned up and planted a kiss on his cheek, whispering, "Morning."

He let out another sigh and rolled onto his side toward me. "A good morning, I'd say."

I laughed softly, tugging the blankets tighter around us. "Are you sure we can't just go back to sleep forever?"

"And miss all the fun?" The way he winked as he said the last word made my stomach do a flip for all the right reasons.

Before I could respond, my phone gave a loud, indignant blare, skittering across the bedside table. Groaning, I blindly made a grab for it, only succeeding in knocking it to the floor. I was intent to leave it, but it levitated into view. I glanced sideways to see Taron holding out a hand, drawing it towards him.

"No, really, you can just ignore it," I protested.

The phone continued to move through mid-air until it settled on the bed between us, and he tapped the option to quiet the alarm. "There, no more distractions."

"You know, you don't have to try so hard to win me over. Newsflash, you've already succeeded."

It was his turn to laugh. "Noted." He set the phone aside and stroked my cheek with the tip of his index finger. "I cannot tell you how much I have relished these last few weeks."

"Me, too."

Just as he leaned in for a kiss, the bloody phone began buzzing again, this time with an incoming call. I mentally cursed the inventor of the cell phone for interfering with my morning cuddle. Letting out an exhale, I picked it up and saw Emerys' face flashing on the screen. I rolled so that I faced away from Taron and answered the call.

"Hello?"

"I did not want to believe Julayne when she told me you'd been sneaking off, but I see she was correct."

"Don't know what you mean."

"Well, unless you have mastered both the ability to turn yourself invisible and mute all sound, you are not in your room."

"How do you know that?"

"Because I am standing in it. The bed has clearly

not been slept in." Annoyance brought out the Irish lilt in her voice.

"I didn't realize I needed permission to visit family property."

Silence on the line lasted all of five seconds before she said, "I wish I could argue with that, yet technically you are correct."

From behind me, I felt Taron's body press against me, his lips trailing kisses along my shoulder. "Not that I don't appreciate the wake-up call, but is there a particular reason you are looking for me?"

"For a modern woman who maintained gainful employment, you are woefully unable to use a calendar," she quipped. "The interview you agreed to, so that the people could get to know their prodigal princess is today."

Shit.

I moved so that I sat upright, blankets artfully covering my torso. It left Taron woefully uncovered, and I couldn't help sneaking a peek at his toned, muscular torso. "But that's hours off."

"There is a lot to be done before the interview even begins. Your mother needs to brief you and then there's wardrobe, accessories ... Just get home. Now."

The finality of her tone as she ended the call reminded me of Aunt Nim's tough mum attitude she'd tried on me as a teenager. It hadn't done much good then either. In that quiet moment, a pang of sadness washed over me.

"I need to go," I announced, setting the phone temporarily back onto the night table.

"Are you certain you can't stay, even just a little longer?" I turned to see him playfully pouting at me.

"Don't pretend you didn't hear that entire conversation. Apparently, it takes five hours to get ready for an interview." Hell, I hadn't spent more than twenty minutes preparing for my job interview to bartend at The Witching Hour. A television one wouldn't be much different.

"Ah, yes. The plight of royal women. Ask Talia about it some time. I am certain she'd commiserate with you."

His nakedness slid from beneath the blankets, striding confidently across the small room to claim his folded trousers, shirt, and boots. He stuffed them into a bag he'd brought with him, signaling he intended to return to his kingdom in his shifted form. The thought of him walking out into the snow stark naked made me cringe, yet he'd assured me he wasn't prone to frostbite.

I tugged on my jeans and a dark grey jumper before moving on to my socks and boots. Leading the way down to the first floor of the cabin, I gave the space a cursory glance. There was evidence we'd lit a fire in the hearth the night before, its embers still smoldering thanks to Taron's assistance. The mugs and other dishes we'd used sat in the sink.

"Give me a few minutes to tidy up," I said, moving into what I considered Gethin's domain.

Even though my friend hadn't been by in nearly a month, I still felt I couldn't leave his space a mess. Scrubbing and rinsing the dishes, I set them on the rack to dry. When I returned to the main room, Taron had snuffed the remaining coals and held the door open. A chilly gust of air blew through and I shivered.

"Next time, I really need to remember a coat," I muttered.

I marched out onto the frozen ground and waited for Taron to take his dragon form. After offering him a quick kiss on the snout, I watched him take flight. I waited until his bulky form was a speck in the distance before I traced a circle mid-air and stepped through the portal back into my bedroom.

I half-expected Emerys to still be standing there

crossly. Though the room was empty. A handwritten note from Emerys reminded me that I should report to my mother's sitting room immediately upon my return. Squaring my shoulders, I left the bedroom and made my way through the corridors. Even though I'd spent more time away from the castle in recent weeks, the place was beginning to feel more familiar with each passing day. I hardly got lost anymore.

"Tea?" my mother asked the moment I stepped into her sitting room. Emerys was conspicuously absent.

"Yeah, tea sounds good," I said and settled in the chair beside her.

She leaned over and brushed a few tiny snowflakes from my hair. "I didn't know it was snowing inside."

"Went for a walk and just got back."

"Hmm. You might want to remember a coat next time."

I coughed into my teacup and didn't make eye contact with her. She studied me a moment longer. "You are a grown woman, as you keep reminding me. I just ask that you try not to cause any diplomatic incidents."

"I don't plan on it."

"Good. Speaking of avoiding diplomatic incidents, we should go through your talking points for today."

"I thought it was just a getting to know me?"

"Well, yes, but it can't be a free for all."

"Don't worry, I wasn't planning to reveal any deep, dark secrets." I sipped from the teacup in my hand and my stomach rumbled with hunger. My mother slid a plate of chocolate chip scones across the table between us. "What sort of things ought I stay away from?"

"Well, they may ask you about the recent cyber-attacks. Just tell them to contact the Crown's press office."

"Seems easy enough."

"They may try to get you to talk about your return to Camelot and the tournament. You don't have to share anything you aren't comfortable with." She held up a printed sheet of paper. "I did vet some of the questions."

She passed it over and I studied the list. They weren't too difficult. Some were downright vapid, like my favorite foods and colors and time of year. I couldn't help but feel the last one was some slight way to make sure I wasn't secretly a spring-loving Seelie. There was also a question near the end about my feelings towards Arthur and his family.

"They aren't really going to ask me about him, are they?"

"Given the circumstances, I don't see a way around it, I'm afraid. Just be cordial."

The image of Arthur gleefully facing off against me in the final bout of the tournament flashed through my mind. *Pompous wanker.* "I promise I won't lose my shit during the interview."

She cleared her throat. "You should refrain from more ... colorful language. You are representing the Crown."

"Again, I thought this was to get to know me. Not some polished up version."

"Even still, we have certain standards we need to uphold."

"I grew up in the city and worked in a bar. There's only so much polish a girl like me can handle." Speaking of ... Emerys mentioned needing hours for wardrobe?"

"A formality, I'm afraid. Eat up and we'll get you on your way."

In the back of my head, I secretly wished some new quest would land in my lap, so I wouldn't have to get primped and pruned like a doll. No such luck by the time I'd finished two scones and another cup of tea. Steeling myself, I followed my mother out of her sitting room and up a short flight of stairs into a brightly lit room with rolling racks of dresses and make-up tables with huge ring lights.

"Your Majesty," a woman with blonde hair braided around her head like a crown said, offering a deep bow as my mother entered. She gave a quicker, second bow as she looked at me. "Your Highness."

"Morgan, I'm sure you've met Brigette. She handles all of our wardrobe needs. You have her to thank for no corsets."

"You know, I'm sure I'll be fine to get my own clothes," I said, trying to take a step out of the room.

"Oh, you can't go out looking like that?" Brigette said dismissively.

"What's wrong with this?" I protested.

"For one thing, it's not a dress."

"Right because princesses only wear dresses," I shot back. "I keep telling you, I'm not some doll to be dressed up." I gestured the length of my body. "You want the people to know me? Well, *this* is me."

"Give us a moment," my mother said, and Brigette offered a quick curtsy before vacating the room.

"I'm not trying to be difficult," I began, but she held up her hand for silence.

"I understand this isn't what you're used to, but we aren't in London. You are not tending bar. You are the heir apparent to this kingdom's throne and that carries certain expectations. Show the people who you are in deeds and words. You can manage wearing a dress for an hour or two."

"I don't have a choice, do I?"

"No."

I let out a long sigh. "Fine."

"Good. Now, I'll see you down there. We'll be setting up in the receiving room just beyond the throne room. It's quiet and intimate."

I forced a smile as she walked out, and Brigette returned. She shut the door and made a gesture signaling I should undress. I tugged the jumper over my head and shimmied out of my jeans. Bridgette assessed me in my underwear in silence for a moment as she rifled through some of the dresses on the racks. Most were long sleeve and floor length. She caught me watching her and moved to a rack where the hem lines was more mid-calf. My shoulders relaxed a little when she finally handed me one in a vibrant blue that melted into a deep purple at the bottom.

"Try this on."

I stepped into the dress, zipping it up at the back. It fit remarkably well and fell flatteringly over my torso. Next, she passed me a slender gold belt that I secured around my waist.

"You actually look pretty good in boots. But those are a bit chunky. Try these." She handed me a pair of slimmer dark grey boots that tapered to a point at the toe and had a half-inch heel. At least I wasn't going to break my neck walking in them. I settled in one of the seats in front of the make-up table as I put them on.

"Can I see your ears?"

My stomach did a flip at her words before I realized she probably just wanted to see if they could accommodate piercings. I brushed my hair behind my ears, and she handed me simple gold studs and a set of hoops. I secured them and studied myself in the chair. It wasn't horrible as looks went. Brigette moved to grab a make-up palette.

"Please don't make me look ridiculous," I begged.

"You're lucky you've got cheekbones and a nice complexion. You don't need much."

I'd have almost said she used magic to apply the blush, eyeliner, and shadow because the brushes were so soft and gentle. When I checked my reflection in the mirror I could see where she'd enhanced my features without overemphasizing them.

"Okay, I definitely misjudged you."

"You're not the first. Now, what to do about your hair."

Our gazes met in the mirror. "Guessing I can't just toss it up in a knot."

"Not if you want them to take you seriously." She held up a slender gold circlet crown. "Besides, we're going to need to secure this."

My mouth went dry. I hadn't worn a crown since coming back to Camelot. Not even when I'd joined my mother for announcements or press. She'd always been the focus. "Get on with it then."

She swept my hair into a loose plait down to my shoulders and secured the crown on my head with two tiny pins. She squinted at me. "Yeah, I think that will do."

With Brigette's blessing, I left the room and headed down to the first floor. The receiving room was ahead of me when I caught sight of Jules and Laoise in the corridor. A month of good food, clean lodgings, and a bath had made the girl far more vibrant. She offered a vigorous wave when she spotted me coming.

"You two look thick as thieves," I said.

"Just practicing our polite society manners," Jules answered. "You look brilliant."

"I feel ridiculous. But I guess that's part of being a princess. Wish me luck."

"You are a hero. You do not need luck," Laoise replied, but gave me a swift hug around the middle.

Leaving the pair behind, I stepped into the receiving room, ready for whatever the reporters threw at me. Let's hope I didn't royally fuck it up.

CHAPTER

TWO

The receiving room was almost silent as I walked in. A camera sat up against one wall, with an operator crouched behind it. He adjusted the lens and some other bits and bobs as I took in the space. Two chairs were seated about three or four feet apart facing the camera. An older woman with a shock of blonde hair already occupied the far seat. She studied something on a tablet, and I cleared my throat to get her attention. She looked up and the tablet nearly fell from her fingers in her haste to stand and offer me a bow.

"Your Highness."

"Really, Morgan's fine."

"Please, sit. We're about ready to begin."

I sucked in a breath and held it for a count of ten

before I moved to take the vacant chair. The lighting overhead was soft, which I suspected was purpose-ful; a way to make the viewing public and me more comfortable. It wasn't some harsh interrogation. I smoothed the hem of the dress nervously as I waited for the woman to actually introduce herself. She remained seated, but the camera operator came over with a lapel microphone and clipped it to my dress collar, snaking the cord down my back and looping it through the belt at my waist.

Oh, how I wished Jules or Gethin could be in the room with me. At least then I could pretend I was just chatting with my mates. But they were both off occupied. Even Rory and Avery were busy gaining their bearings in the castle and surrounding area.

"We're ready," the camera operator called in a gruff bass tone.

The woman settled her tablet back in her lap and leaned over. "Don't be nervous, Your Highness. I've done hundreds of interviews."

Her insistence on being overly formal grated my nerves and did nothing to settle my unease. "I've never been interviewed like this before. I don't want to say or do the wrong thing."

"Oh, we'll be editing things out," she said with a dismissive handwave.

Her assurance didn't instill me with confidence either. Sure, my mother would likely have final approval over whatever was broadcast, but I knew all too well how editing could change the context of a person's words.

"Look, you want to make me more comfortable? Start with just calling me Morgan."

"Right. Of course." She held out her hand for me to shake. "And my apologies for not introducing myself right away when you came in. My name is Davida Shaw."

I shook her hand in as firm a grip as I could muster. "Nice to meet you."

Davida tucked a few loose strands of blonde hair behind her ear as she angled herself toward me. She gave the camera operator a nod and I could see the record light flip on.

"Good morning, Camelot. This is Davida Shaw. I am here in the heart of Camelot's royal residence to give you all an exclusive intimate chat with our kingdom's Crown Princess." She turned to me. "Thank you for sitting down with us, Princess."

I forced a smile. "Happy to. And please, do call me Morgan. All my friends do."

She let out a hiccup of laughter. "Well, we

haven't even started and we're already friends. I like that."

I continued to hold the smile as I caught the camera panning between us. Davida looked down at her tablet and said, "Many of our viewers don't know your story, or they've only heard what's been released officially by the crown. Why don't you tell us what life was like for you, raised outside of nobility?"

I shrugged, causing feedback on the microphone. "I didn't really have a choice in the matter. But my Aunt Nim brought me to London and raised me as her own. We lived a quiet life. I went to primary and secondary school. I had a best mate from the time I was five years old, and I was just ... normal. Nothing special."

"It certainly sounds like quite the rags to riches story."

"I mean, I heard stories growing up about Camelot and that one day I might rule it. But I was just a kid, and I had questions about where I came from. Part of me always thought my aunt just told me those stories to make me feel like I mattered to someone other than just her."

"This aunt you talk about, she was the woman who took you away from your family?"

I shifted in the seat, trying to put distance between us as her tone rubbed me the wrong way. "She was a good person. She saved my life. If she hadn't been brave enough to stand up against what she knew was wrong, I'd have died the day I was born. I owe her my life." I turned and looked straight down the center of the camera lens. "She was forced into a horrible situation, and she made the best of it. And she paid the ultimate price for it. She was murdered and I will do everything I can to see her get the justice she deserves."

Davida didn't make eye contact with me as she scrolled through whatever questions she'd prepared. I took the brief pause in the conversation to pull back on my anger starting to bubble to the surface. It always seemed to come any time I thought about Nim's death lately. I hated that the Seelie bastards who'd taken her life had never seen justice, not really. And the fucker behind the whole plan sat safe and secure in his own castle. Untouchable.

"Let's go back to your life before you found yourself in Camelot. You had a career. Tell us, what sort of aspirations did you have?"

"I was a bartender. I can make almost any drink you can imagine. Some you probably haven't even heard of. I didn't ever intend to do it, not for as long as I did anyway. But it was something I was good at. Something I didn't have to do with the expectation that I needed to be great. It was a simple life."

"It sounds like you were comfortable in that world where no one knew your truth."

"It's what made me who I am. I wouldn't trade that." I realized as the words left my mouth how that might come across as a dig at my mother and the life she could have offered me here in the castle. "What I mean is the things I went through shaped me and I honestly don't know who I'd be."

Keep digging the hole deeper, why don't you, Morgan?

"Maybe we should talk about something else," I said rubbing at the nape of my neck.

"Why don't we talk about what led to you bursting into our lives? That tournament was certainly something to behold."

"I winged most of it, if I'm honest." I wanted to tell her how much Aunt Nim had prepared me for the challenge without realizing it, but I could sense bringing her up again wasn't the right move. "I was grateful for the chance to participate and that I was found worthy of the victor's trophy."

"So, you didn't know you'd be unseating a rival prince?"

I let out an involuntary laugh. "Before the tournament, I'd never even met that pompous prat. I don't know how much he knew about what he was doing, but he's still complicit in causing turmoil to my family."

Davida gave another small laugh; like she was enjoying the anger in my voice. "You may not have been raised in Camelot, but I see its views have ingrained themselves in you already."

I gripped the edge of the chair to keep from launching myself across the room at her. Instead, I turned to look at the camera operator. "Turn it off."

"We're not finished," Davida countered.

"I'm the fucking Crown Princess. Turn it off."

I flung out a hand and sparks flew from the camera as the record light died and the operator jumped back. I was on my feet and rounded on Davida. "You might think you're playing some clever game, but you're full of shit. You think I don't see what you're doing?"

She batted her lashes at me, as if playing dumb. "I don't know what you mean."

"You didn't want to get to know me. You wanted to talk me into a corner I couldn't get out of. You wanted to stoke the tensions between us and the Seelie."

"I've interviewed a lot of royals in my time. None have been so rude."

I let out a bitter laugh. "You want to report something on me? Here you go; I'm not one for frilly dresses and fancy manners. I'm a working-class girl who swears like a sailor. Now, this interview's over."

I yanked the lapel microphone off my collar and tugged the cord until it came loose before tossing it on the chair and throwing the door wide open.

"Well, I suppose it shouldn't surprise you that Uther's annual Winter Solstice Ball invitations went out, and you weren't on the list," Davida called.

"Wouldn't have gone anyway." I whirled to face her. "Don't expect to ever get another interview from this family again."

I stormed out of the room and wound my way towards the kitchens, hoping I'd find Gethin. He could make my irritation recede with a delicious meal. The room was bustling with activity, but my friend was nowhere to be seen. I caught the sleeve of one of the chefs as he was setting a large three-layer cake onto a stand for icing.

"Sorry, you haven't seen Gethin have you?"

He shook his head. "He hasn't been down this morning, Highness."

"Damn. Thanks anyway."

I made it halfway back to the corridor that would take me to throne room when I felt a presence behind me. I stopped walking, forcing every muscle to remain still as I waited for something to happen.

"You really do not know how to not pick a fight, Morgan?" Emerys' voice came from the shadows behind me.

Tension ebbed from my shoulders as I turned to face her. "Oh, you heard about that already?"

She gave me a wry grin. "The Crown Princess storming out of an interview while shouting profanity is not something staff are bound to miss."

"She completely set me up. She was supposed to not get all political and just pushed me into it."

"Your mother will be dealing with her. But you shouldn't have risen to the bait."

"What, did you want me to lie? Not to say that Nim deserves justice for being brutally murdered and that we all know Uther was behind it?'

"We may know the circumstances, but at this point, it is your word against his. And he is a master of manipulation, if your thirty-year absence is anything to judge by."

"So what, will it just not air?"

"I can't say what your mother will do, but I assume not."

"I tried, I really did, to be all proper and diplomatic. But I just couldn't. It's not me."

"You should not have to change who you are to be the leader this kingdom needs. You were correct in saying that your experiences shaped you."

"You heard that bit?"

She nodded. "I may have been listening by the door." She reached up and touched the gold crown still pinned in my hair. "It does suit you, though."

"I still feel like an imposter." I moved to lean against one of the stone walls, a sconce illuminating the space around me. "As much as I hate to admit it, that prick is better at all this royal stuff than me."

"Enough wallowing. This isn't anything we cannot come back from. Chin up."

Silence fell between us for a moment and the edges of my anger dulled more. "What's this Solstice Ball she was on about?"

"Usually, Uther hosts one in the spring. But since the Unseelie court fell off the political stage, he swooped into take over the festivities."

"How does an entire kingdom just fall off the political map?"

"They have always been mercurial and keep to themselves. We received word that they were closing their borders, and we've respected that for many years now."

"She acted like it was some big offense I wasn't invited. Like I would have gone anyway. I think we all know I couldn't have stopped myself from punching that twat in the throat."

"Even when tensions have been high, that courtesy has always been extended. I have little doubt Uther is trying to show off his influence by barring Camelot's court from attending."

Before I could tell her that I wasn't offended by the exclusion, heat rippled from my chest across my shoulders and down into my belly. Air fled my lungs and if I hadn't already been leaning against the wall, I'd have fallen over. As it was, I pressed my left hand flat against the stone, praying I'd remain upright as I tried to process what was going on. The fabric of the dress Brigitte had picked out for me started to smolder and smoke. I reached beneath the collar to extract the compass. It burned against the pads of my fingers and yet I couldn't pull them away.

Suddenly, the corridor vanished, and I saw flashes of a gleaming black archer's bow, ornate and elegant strung up on a pristine white wall. The air was sweet with the scent of something floral I couldn't name. It promised danger even as the bow called out to me. A black banner flashed before the images vanished and I found myself back in the corridor, Emerys at my side.

"What happened? What did you see?"

I managed to pry my fingers from the compass' metal covering and shook them out to dispel the residual pain. Phantom white hot spots still made my joints ache when I flexed my hand. "An archer's bow. It was all black and I don't know why, but it felt like it was somewhere dangerous. I couldn't see any real landmarks. Just a black bit of a banner."

"It would seem another quest has laid itself out before you."

Brilliant. Just what I wanted. Why did being a hero have to be filled with so many bloody quests?

"Better assemble the troops then. Something tells me we don't have a lot of time to waste."

CHAPTER

THREE

Rallying the troops happened faster than I'd expected. I sent a group text to Gethin, Rory, Avery, and Jules to meet in my mother's sitting room. It wasn't the most spacious of places, but it was secluded, and we weren't likely to be overheard. Ten minutes later, I sat in one of the plush chairs, tugging pins free and setting the circlet crown down on the small table beside me. Emerys had made additional chairs materialize as my friends crammed in.

"So, what's going on?" Rory sounded genuinely excited by her inclusion in the group huddle.

"Is this where you tell us how well the interview went?" Gethin sounded hopeful.

"Well, if it were good news, she wouldn't have used so many periods," Jules noted.

I sucked in a breath before saying, "The interview was utter shit. That lady totally blindsided me. But that's not the reason for this meeting. I had a vision."

"Vision? Like, the kind that sends you off on quests?" The hint of excitement in Jules' voice was unmistakable.

"That's the one."

"What are we after this time? More jewelry?" Avery leaned against the makeshift bar at the back of the room. She absently brushed a finger over the pendant at her throat. She hadn't taken it off since she'd settled in at the castle.

"More weapons it would seem. It looked like an archer's bow."

"What sort of bow?" Jules' eyes sparkled. I could feel the wave of excitement wafting from her. I couldn't blame her. She had felt a little left out after our most recent trip through the barrier. If I had any choice, I'd have her at my side on every quest that lay ahead from here on out.

"Probably easier to just show you."

No one questioned what I meant. Instead, they all sat perfectly still and watched me in silence. I closed my eyes and felt the core of my magic spark to life as I turned my attention inward. I pictured the image of the shiny, sleek bow I'd seen when the compass had nearly set me on fire and projected it into the space in front of me. Opening my eyes, I was pleased to find it floating mid-air between myself and Rory.

"Looks kind of unremarkable," Rory offered.

"Looks so ... pristine," Gethin murmured.

"What do you mean?" I moved to study the object from his vantage point. It was certainly clean. Yet I got the sense he had more to say on the matter and made a gesture for him to continue.

"It's just that the other objects you've had to find have all been old, powerful relics in a sense. This looks like it could have been fashioned far more recently."

"An object's appearance does not necessarily convey it's age, or its power," Emerys noted from where she stood sentinel at the door.

"Did you get a sense of where this bow might be hiding?" Avery pushed off the bar to stand beside me. She poked at the floating magical memory version of the bow.

"All I could see was a bit of black fabric. Nothing overly descriptive."

"Hang on, what's that along the outer edge?" Avery bent close and traced her finger along the length of the bow. When she stepped back, a faint orange trail remained illuminating a series of symbols and what looked like the image of a sword.

"Oh, that's ancient Seelie," Gethin piped up. I spun to face my friend. "Please tell me that's one of the languages you've studied?"

He adjusted his glasses. "A little. Honestly, the grammar is downright confusing." I watched as he bent closer, his mouth working to form words. "I haven't read up on it in a while, but it almost looks like ... the Seelie coat of arms motto for the royal family."

My heart plummeted into my stomach. Ancient Seelie writing. The royal family's motto. Glimpses of black fabric. My mind flashed back to right after Arthur's jail break and the broadcast Uther had made from his throne room, flanked by the tall black banners.

"Oh, fuck no."

"Morgan." Emerys' voice came sharp and warning. "You cannot enter their kingdom, especially not intending to take things that may very well be theirs by right."

I looked at her. "You think I want to go there? I'd

rather gouge my own eyeballs out than set foot anywhere near them."

"Are we absolutely certain that's where you're supposed to go? I mean, Gethin did just admit he's rusty," Rory interjected. "Maybe he was just reading it wrong."

Gethin glowered at her. "I may be a little out of practice, but I can recognize their motto thank you very much. Besides, no one but a Seelie would put that on a weapon. Any chance it's just sitting in a collector's shop or something?"

"Given everything that's happened in the last few months, are you sure you even want to do this?" Avery pivoted to face me. "I understand you feel called, but maybe something's different about this time."

"Different how?"

She shrugged. "What if you're not meant to go after this … What if it's a test to see if you can actually know when it's right to go traipsing into someone else's kingdom? A good leader needs to know how to navigate precarious political situations and this could be a really good way to see if you're able to read those signals."

I tugged the compass from beneath my dress' collar again. "This nearly burned me with its insistence to show me this bloody bow. I'm not ignoring it."

"You need to be smart about what you do next is all I'm saying."

"Maybe the timing is perfect." Jules began pacing. "They don't think Morgan would show up and Uther will be busy with the festivities. It would be an excellent time to slip in and grab the bow."

"Jules, when has any of this been easy?"

"We could do it. Just the pair of us," she proclaimed, casting looks at Rory and Avery. "No offense to either of you. It just feels like we're meant to do this together."

"I don't even know where to begin on something like this, Jules. Of course I want you with me, but we have to be smart about it. We need to do some research, maybe even some recon first before we decide our next steps." I didn't add how it seemed with each quest I was destined to add another knight to my growing army. I couldn't exactly do that with just Jules at my side.

"You will not be setting foot in their kingdom, regardless of who accompanies you. Your mother will not allow it, and neither will I," Emerys protested. "If you must seek this weapon, it has to be done another way. One that does not put your life in immediate jeopardy."

"What if Julayne's right and you use the big party as a distraction?" Rory proposed, a mischievous look on her face. "I'm sure you know someone who got an invite who'd be happy to take you. And be keen to watch your back, too."

The way she waggled her eyebrows at me told me exactly who she meant. And it wasn't a half-bad idea. But that would mean getting both my mother and Emerys' blessing as well as the King and Queen of the Dragon Court.

"I could ask Taron if he got an invite. I can't promise he'd be willing to risk it, but it's worth a shot. What good are allies if we can't lean on them once and a while."

Jules shot me a look that clearly communicated she'd applied innuendo to my words. I rolled my eyes at her implied unspoken naughtiness before retrieving my phone and sending Taron a text.

> Hey, I've got a favor to ask of you.
> Might be best if both you and Talia
> come by.

His reply came almost instantly, as if he spent all

of his time glued to his phone hoping I'd send him a missive.

> Let's hope this one doesn't involve quite so much death.

My stomach contorted with a tinge of guilt at his words. I tried to discern a hint of playfulness and sarcasm in his words. Though at the moment, I regretted not just calling him. It was so much simpler to judge tone that way.

I looked at my assembled group of friends. "No matter what we end up doing, we'll need to know what we're walking into. This ball is in two days. We don't have a lot of time." I gestured to Avery. "You see what you can find about the layout of the Seelie castle. Anything about the floorplan or construction. Maybe there's something in Camelot's archives or military files." To Jules, I added, "And you, Gethin, and Rory see what you can dig up on any references to this bow." Before I stopped fueling the spell, I took a closer look at the texture of the bow. "It looks like it's got something like obsidian in the design. Start there."

"What are you going to do?"

"Try and convince my mother that this quest isn't going to absolutely blow up in our faces. And persuade some dragons to help break us into the season's most exclusive event."

I left the room and went in search of my mother. I found her in the Council room, sitting alone at the head of the rectangular table. She appeared lost in thought, and I had to knock on the door twice to draw her attention.

"Sorry to interrupt you," I said, standing in the doorway.

Her gaze found mine and I expected her to be angry with me for blowing up the interview with Davida. Instead, her face softened. "I am so sorry about what happened with that interview."

"It's not like it got broadcast," I said dismissively. "I came by because I needed to talk to you about something else. It's important and dangerous."

She sat up in her seat and folded her hands on the table in front of her. "That doesn't sound good."

"You know how I've been having these sort of ... uh, quests lately. Bringing the Amber Chalice back to Camelot. Finding Avery and Rory, and the pendant and the shield to help protect the kingdom?"

She nodded wordlessly.

"Well, it looks like I've got another one and this time it's, uh ... in Seelie territory."

"That is not a place you want to be right now."

I swallowed the lump in my throat. "It gets worse. I think what I'm meant to find is in their castle."

"If you are found there, they would have every right to detain you. Morgan, the Seelie could execute you."

"I know. Believe me, everyone's been telling me how stupid it would be to go. But I can't shake the idea that I have to be there." I moved deeper into the room and took a seat beside her. "I've got everyone looking into what we're up against before we make any decisions. Taron and Talia are coming here. I'm hoping maybe they could help me sort things out."

"I know the dragons have long been our allies, but you put a great deal of faith in them."

I hadn't shared the news of mine and Taron's relationship with my mother yet. It was still so new, I wanted it to be just for the pair of us. Instead, I said, "Taron faced a lot of things from his past in Dublin. He could have just flat out ignored me or abandoned me when it turned out his mentor was a raving purist murderer. But he stuck by me. He proved himself as someone I can trust. And I do."

"I am beginning to understand that I cannot stop you when you set your mind to something."

I smirked. "Yeah, Aunt Nim said that a lot, too, when I was little. Called me the world's most stubborn child."

"I refuse to believe that I have just gotten you back only to lose you again so soon." She reached out and grasped my right hand in hers. "Be careful daughter."

Just then, my phone buzzed with another text from Taron, letting me know they'd arrived.

"Well, I better see if I can convince them to help."

ON MY WAY TO meet Talia and Taron, I swung by the library and pulled Gethin from his research duties, leaving Jules and Rory to continue digging. We met our dragon guests in the front corridor and brought them into the same receiving room I'd used for my ill-fated interview with Davida.

"So, I'm guessing you got an invite for Uther's Solstice Ball, right?" I said, launching headfirst into the discussion once the door was closed.

"I'm surprised you know about that," Talia answered.

"Until an hour ago, I didn't. But it would appear that it's going to be the event of the season. I'm not invited, but I need to get in ... somehow."

"I think I like where this is going." Talia's eyes twinkled with excitement. "I guess I'll be responding as a yes this year."

"You're not going," Taron said.

Talia whirled to face her brother, and I was reminded just how fierce she could be. Her entire body flashed orange as she got in his face. "Since when do you dictate where I go?"

"Since you'd be walking into enemy territory where they wouldn't think twice about assassinating the heir apparent of a foreign power."

"I'm sure they wouldn't be that brazen," I offered, trying to divert some of the hostility away from Taron.

"Says the princess who was nearly murdered at birth and replaced with an imposter," Talia snapped before all the fire went out of her. "I didn't mean that."

"Yeah, you did and it's fine. You aren't wrong. I don't have a say in any of this."

"I know I have no right to dictate your movements, but you shouldn't go either," Taron continued, his tone gentler.

"Believe me, I don't fancy being anywhere near the Seelie when they've got home field advantage, but the compass clearly pointed me there. And if I've learned anything over the last few months with these quests, it's that I'm meant to be there for a reason."

"Fine, Taron can go to represent the royal family," Talia sighed. She jabbed a finger in my direction. "And you'll be there, too. Just not ... you."

"I don't follow."

"What are the Seelie exceptionally good at?" Taron had caught on to whatever his sister was proposing.

"Being obnoxious, entitled arseholes?"

"Try hiding in plain sight," Talia replied.

"Oh, I think I know what you're suggesting," Gethin piped up from across the room.

I raised my hand. "Someone want to fill me in?"

"If I'm right, they're going to use some shifter magic to change your appearance and pass you off as one of them," Gethin answered, excitement bubbling in his tone.

"I knew I liked him," Talia said with a wink that made Gethin's cheeks burn pink.

"This all sounds good in theory, but the minute Morgan tries to do magic, they'll realize she's not one of you," Gethin noted.

"Leave it to me," Talia said and leaned over, wrapping an arm around my shoulder. "You're going to make a brilliant dragon."

"Just as long as I don't have to transform into one. No offense, you're both bloody brilliant in either form, but it kind of freaks me out."

"I promise, you won't have any reason to go that far," Taron said, fixing me with a protective look that momentarily quelled my fears.

CHAPTER

FOUR

The beginnings of a plan were now in motion. I had to trust Talia would handle what I needed to sneak into the Seelie court unnoticed. Now, I needed to gather all the information I could about what we were facing. But first, I accompanied Taron and Talia back to the front gates of the castle.

"I truly appreciate all the help you've given me the last few months." I held out a hand to Talia.

She arched a brow at me before shaking it. "Us Crown Princesses have to stick together." Her grip tightened on mine, and she pulled me forward so she could whisper in my ear. "Besides, I like to keep my brother's romantic prospects under close observation."

My jaw worked to form words. Taron and I had

sworn we'd tell no one of our burgeoning relationship. "We're not ..."

Talia laughed. "Oh, he didn't have to say a word. I know my brother well and I can see when his mood brightens. Any mentions of you bring it out in him. I just made the logical deduction from there."

My cheeks flushed. "It's just ... it's new. We're still figuring things out."

"Your secret is safe with me. But you should be damn sure you're willing to commit if he is. Because you might think you know what it means to be loved by a man, but I can guarantee you've never held the eye and heart of a dragon."

I couldn't argue with that. I also couldn't help picking up on the sense of danger that laced her words. But there wasn't time to press her further. Taron gestured for her to join him as they stepped out into the wintry courtyard.

"We will return tomorrow with everything we need. Be ready," he called, the wind drawing his words out into the world and away from me.

Nothing like a deadline to motivate a girl.

I spun on my heel to find Gethin waiting for me. "I know I seemed okay with this plan just now, but I can't let you go without telling you it terrifies me. Even if Talia is as good as she thinks she is, you will be surrounded by people who want to kill you. You could run into Arthur. Or Uther."

"I know, mate. I don't have all the answers yet. That's why we need to see what the girls have found on the castle and this bow. Come on. Let's get pulled in on the research."

We wound our way back to the library. I couldn't help but flash back to the last time I'd been within these walls with Gethin and Taron searching for information on the Syndicate's history. I'd never really been the studious type. But Jules lived for places like this. When I found her seated at one of the tables with books strewn around her, I was reminded just how much she was in her element. Rory sat beside her, skimming through the pages of an oversized tome.

Avery sat a few tables away, fingers flying over the keyboard of a laptop that sported Camelot's crest where the usual brand logo would be on the case.

"So, we think we've got a lead on a plan to get me in there," I said softly, drawing the three women's attention.

"It better be damn near perfect, because one wrong move and we'll be down one very necessary royal," Jules said, looking up from her notes.

"I'll be attending the festivities, but just not as myself. In fact, I'll be hiding amongst the dragon contingent. I don't have all the details about how I'll accomplish it. But I trust our allies will pull it off."

"That's actually really smart," Rory said.

Jules' nose wrinkled in disagreement. "It's become pretty obvious that Camelot and the dragons are back on good terms. Wouldn't the Seelie expect them to pull something to help Camelot?"

"While I appreciate you playing devil's advocate Jules, I really need all the positive vibes I can get right now. We just have to hope that Uther is so focused on putting on a show for his guests that I can fly under the radar." I gestured to the array of books. "Please tell me you've found something on this bow."

"There are a surprising number of obsidian-related weapons," Rory piped up and offered me a scrap of paper with a list of various objects ranging from knives to maces to archery bows, all with references to obsidian. "A lot of them seem to be more descriptors, like it's as dark as obsidian, rather than having any of the stone in the weapon. But based on the description we're going off of, I think it's this one."

She passed me one of the large texts, opened to a

page with an inked drawing of the bow. I settled in one of the other chairs around the table and read the short passage aloud. "The Obsidian Bow is said to have been crafted nearly one thousand years ago at the birth of the Seelie empire. It is said to contain mystical properties to obscure the wielder from their enemies and any arrow loosed from the weapon will find its true target."

Brilliant. In the wrong hands, this one weapon could take out an army.

No wonder Uther had the weapon hanging in his castle. The king would want to keep an eye on the bow and know it hadn't sprouted legs and wandered off into *his* enemies hands.

"Any other mentions of it being used in battle? How'd Uther get his hands on it?"

I had no real sense of how old Uther was. He could have been my mother's age, or he could have been hundreds of years old like Emerys or even Gaius de Burn. Seelies were long-lived like dragons.

"There's a couple of later references that the original craftsman was a Seelie noble who gifted it to the royal family as a sign of devotion and loyalty," Rory continued.

"Pretty sure the king then used it to kill the

maker, so they couldn't craft any more. One of a kind item and all," Jules noted.

"So much for loyalty," I muttered.

"Does it surprise you?" I'd nearly forgotten Gethin stood on Jules' other side.

"No, not really." I set the book down and rubbed the bridge of my nose. "So, we know what it does. At least allegedly anyway and that it's been in the Seelie royal family's possession for longer than my family has ruled this kingdom. Is there anything about ... I don't know, booby traps or other ways they've used to secure it all this time? I don't believe for a second we're the first people thinking of nicking it off Uther."

"I'm sure there must be, but no one's around to write about that," Jules scoffed. "They'd all be dead."

"She's right. I doubt the Seelie would publicize the ways their enemies failed to obtain this insanely powerful weapon," Rory agreed.

"Ugh! There's got to be something," I sighed and turned my attention to Avery. "Any luck on your end?"

"I mean, I've got a few crude renderings of a layout from what looks like a couple hundred years ago. I can't say how accurate they are. And there's every possibility they've changed things around since this was drawn."

"Let me see it."

She passed the laptop over and I balanced it atop the open book. The castle appeared to be situated on a hill and built with polished white stone. Below the image was a black and white sketch of the castle showing three floors. The interior layout was roughly sketched in with notes scribbled next to question marks. I could see what might have been a receiving hall near the front, along with a sitting room of some sort. The throne room looked to be the largest on the first floor and the most obvious one that had no question of its location. The lower level housed what were likely prison cells or a dungeon, along with the kitchens and servants' quarters. The upper floor housed bedrooms. None were labeled as the King's quarters though. Whoever had made this map likely didn't get close enough to find out that level of detail.

It would have to do. I took out my phone and snapped a photo of the screen.

"I could maybe write some code that could possibly give us a more accurate layout once you're actually in the castle," Avery offered.

"Could you do it in the next sixteen hours?

Because Taron and Talia will be here tomorrow to set things in motion."

Avery cracked her knuckles and motioned for me to pass the laptop back to her. "Only one way to find out." With a deep breath, she looked at the rest of our contingent. "I'm going to need some quiet to work."

I grabbed Rory and Jules' notes about the bow, along with the photo of the page from the book. From there I lead the way out of the library and back toward the sleeping quarters.

"I know you'll have the dragons with you, but you shouldn't do this alone," Rory said. "One of us should be with you."

"I know." Eagerness shone bright in her young face. "I need Jules with me on this one. She's someone who has had my back and gotten me out of scrapes before."

Rory hid her disappointment remarkably well. "Just let me know what I can do from here. I can't code like Avery or anything, but I'm sure there's something I can do."

"The minute I know, I'll tell you ..." I paused before adding, "If you happen to have any prophetic dreams, give me a head's up, yeah?"

"You got it."

"I just want you both to be safe," Gethin said, giving me a quick embrace before doing the same to Jules.

"I appreciate it, mate, but we aren't going until tomorrow. No need to get all emotional now."

He pushed his glasses up on his nose. "Yeah, well you never know, when the Seelie are involved."

"Look, I promised Laoise I'd give her one more manners lesson today. And she said she wanted to show me something. I'll see you both later for supper," Jules said.

I didn't know what to do with myself now that we'd figured out and set the beginnings of our plan into proper motion. I had to be patient and bloody hated waiting. But it wouldn't do to show up on the Seelies' doorstep ahead of the festivities and arouse suspicion. In the end, I found myself back upstairs where Brigitte had made me presentable for my interview. I didn't expect to find her, but she sat in front of the mirror, the ring light casting a warm glow over her face as she applied eye shadow expertly on her own lids.

"Oh, sorry," I said, taking a step out of the room.

She set the makeup brush down and waved me in. "You're allowed to be in here. You're the princess, I'd wager you're allowed to be anywhere you want."

"Not if you ask the Council. When we got hacked, they practically told me I wasn't allowed in the chamber."

"Well, they're a bunch of stuffy prats," she said with a wide grin.

"Not all of them." I tugged at the hem of the dress. "Anyway, I thought I'd return this."

"Keep it. The dress looks quite good on you." She tapped her hair. "I do need that crown back though."

I reached up only to remember that I'd taken it off in my mother's sitting room. "Oh, damn. I'll get it."

"You know, I hope the people really like your interview. Once they get to see you're just a normal person, I think they'll come around."

"Yeah, well, I don't think the interview aired since it was a bloody set up. She kept pushing me into answering questions she knew would piss me off or make me look bad."

"Davida? Doesn't sound like her. She's a fair journalist and has always been keen on the crown."

"Couldn't prove it by me. It almost felt as if her questions were all designed to stoke tensions between us and the Seelie. Like she was hoping I'd trip up and she could use it against me somehow."

"Well, you don't have to worry. If it was really that bad, the queen won't let it get out."

That was the hope. I hooked a thumb over my shoulder toward the corridor behind me. "Want to come with me to get the crown? Maybe join us for supper?"

"That's kind of you. But I've got plans tonight." She gestured to the flair of her lashes and the striking eyeliner along her lower lids.

"Hot date?"

She smiled again. "Something like that. I think this might be it. The big proposal. And if she doesn't, I may just have to ask her myself."

"Cheers."

She stood and allowed me to lead her into the corridor. "But I probably should go with you to get the crown. Just to make sure it gets back to its proper place."

We walked in companionable silence to my mother's sitting room. Thankfully, the crown sat on the tiny table exactly where I'd left it. I needed to be more careful with such priceless objects in future. Absently, I rubbed at the band around my left wrist. At least I'd managed not to lose Excalibur on any of my adventures.

"One crown," I said, laying the circlet in her outstretched hand.

Before she could thank me, Gethin appeared at the far end of the corridor. The speed with which he barreled toward us told me something wasn't right. He skidded to a stop and his glasses nearly fell off his nose.

"You need to come with me. Now."

"Take a breath, mate. What's going on?"

"It's Julayne."

He didn't need to say anything more. Brigitte made a frantic shooing gesture when I looked at her, as if giving me permission to abandon her there. I was hot on Gethin's heels as he led me down a flight of stairs and into an open space with dummies and blunted weaponry for soldiers to practice their combat skills. I hadn't been in there much since I'd arrived. As far as I knew, Jules hadn't spent time here either.

Yet, my best friend lay sprawled on the floor at the center of the room, her skin deathly white. Laoise stood off to one side, tears in her eyes as her hands worried the hem of her tunic. I fell to my knees at Jules' side, feeling for a pulse. I found it in her wrist, thrumming slowly, but steadily.

"What happened?"

"It was an accident," the girl said.

Jules' words about the child wanting to show something off came back to me. I tamped down on my anger and looked at Laoise. "Tell me."

She pointed to a slender shield laying on the floor next to Jules. "I was showing her what I could do with it and ... it fell. The shield knocked her down and she did not get up again."

FIVE

Being knocked down by a shield shouldn't have left Jules motionless on the ground. I checked around her head and neck for any obvious signs of trauma, but there was none. I spotted a small cut on her left upper arm and another one on her right forearm that looked as if it could have lined up from an attempt to block the shield from hitting her. I turned and looked at Gethin. "Get a doctor or a medic. Get *someone*."

Without a word, he took off out of sight. I inhaled a slow breath, trying to control the panic rising in me at the sight of my friend so helpless. I reminded myself that we'd been through worse scrapes and had always come out on the other side. Besides, she had a constant pulse and would be fine.

And then a dizzying thought struck me. Laoise had made a very powerful, magical shield before. In fact, she seemed to have been gifted with that particular talent by the universe. I counted to ten in my head before facing the girl. I could see from the way she held herself that she was terrified. She'd been locked up in a cave for so long, starved of normal human interaction. And I'd offered her a place to be free. If I were in her shoes, I'd be pretty scared I was about to find myself out on the street.

"I need to understand more about what happened before she ended up like this." I fought to keep my voice calm and even.

"I made it for her and wanted her to see it. It can prevent an attack from more than one side," Laoise answered, not making eye contact with me.

"You said it fell on her. Like from above, is that right?" She nodded. "How'd it get up there in the first place?"

Her fingers dug deeper into the fabric of her tunic. "I, uh, made it do so."

I reached over and lifted the shield, expecting it to be heavy. After all it had taken Jules out. Except it was lighter than my laptop computer, slender, too. It bore Camelot's coat of arms, capturing the light in a burnished metal sort of way.

"Is it supposed to be heavy?"

Laoise shook her head. "Only if it were to fall into unworthy hands. It was meant to render them unable to use it."

"Clever." Clearly something in her design had gone wrong if it rendered Jules into this state. I set the shield on the floor. "I know you didn't mean to hurt her."

"She is my friend." Laoise was on the verge of tears.

"She's mine, too." The door opened, as the doctor and two nurses barged in, carrying a host of medical contraptions I didn't recognize. They descended on Jules, prodding her and assessing her for injury. Gethin stood just outside the doorway. The way he held his arms wrapped tight around his torso signaled just how worried he was about Jules, too. Without preamble, the two nurses hoisted her into the air, a gurney materializing from thin air beneath her motionless body as they whisked her away.

"Is there anything else you can think of that might help the doctors make her better?" I gave the child's shoulder a firm squeeze.

"I do not know."

"Is there anything special about the things you

used to make the shield?" Gethin offered from his perch just outside the practice room.

Her brow furrowed in thought for a moment. "I used silver, iron, and steel to make it strong."

"I'll let them know," Gethin said, disappearing from view again.

"Come on, let's get you something to eat and take your mind off of things," I told the girl, leading her from the room.

In the back of my mind, I couldn't help but worry that our plans were about to get thrown out of whack. We convened in the dining room, and I did my best to focus on the food before me. But every time I glanced at the chair that had become Jules' seat, my stomach flipped and bile rose in my throat. I couldn't bring myself to eat until I knew Jules would be all right.

"I've heard from the court medical staff that Julayne is under observation," my mother said, drawing my focus from pushing the bits of roast beef around my plate.

"Yes. There was an accident," I answered, not looking at her.

"Well, I'm sure she'll be back on her feet in no time. They mended you right up after the tournament after all."

I wanted to point out that I hadn't been assaulted by a magical weapon. Just beaten up by her imposter son. I held my tongue. Besides, I had more news to share that would no doubt upset her.

"There's something else we need to discuss."

Rory met my gaze across the table and set her utensils down. Gethin did the same.

"By your tone, I take it that whatever it is, it's not going to be something I like," my mother noted.

"No. Definitely not. I know you told me to stay away from the Seelie, but we don't have a choice. I've been given another quest. And the thing we're after is in the heart of the Seelie castle."

"I've already told her this is unwise," Emerys chimed in.

"I'm not going as myself. If all goes well, they won't even know I've been there at all."

"You underestimate our enemy's cunning," my mother murmured.

"Believe me, if I had any other choice, I wouldn't go. But I don't think any of us wants me to ignore the universe."

"You cannot go alone," Emerys added.

"Don't plan to. Remember, I'll have Taron there. And if Jules isn't better by tomorrow, then Rory will have my back." I caught Rory give a small fist pump at the potential chance to tag along before she got her emotions in check. "And Avery is going to have our backs from here. I promise, I'm not going to end up in a dungeon or anything."

"See that you don't." Emerys looked more irritated than I'd seen her in all the time I'd known her.

I looked at my mother now. She was tracing the rim of her water glass with her index finger, as if lost in thought. "I'll only be gone for a few days. The ball lasts a couple days and I don't plan to stay beyond that. If we can't get what we need within that time, then we abandon the whole thing. But once I'm back, we can find someone to do a proper interview so the people can get to know me for real this time."

"I will hold you to that. And I think perhaps it should be a joint affair. Just to make sure things don't go off the rails," my mother answered.

"I'm good with that."

Now I just had to make it through the next day without losing my mind.

I BARELY SLEPT THAT NIGHT. Every time I closed my eyes, I saw Jules laying on the floor, so pale and immobile. By five o'clock, I gave up trying to rest and dressed in the predawn light. I crept through the castle, even though I was home and had every right to be here. At least until I made it to the medical wing. To my surprise, a guard sat just outside Jules' bed. The curtains pulled tight around it. The guard sat up as I approached, his gaze moving over me until he got to my face and recognition struck him.

He was on his feet in an instant, saluting me. "Your Highness."

"Not that I'm not grateful my best mate's got an armed guard at her bedside ... but uh, why does she have an armed guard at her bedside?"

"Queen's orders."

I'd have to ask my mother about it later since it was definitely not something we'd discussed. She'd just been in an accident and Laoise wasn't really at fault. It wasn't like someone was trying to hurt Jules.

"Do you know if she's woken up yet?"

He shook his head. "Sorry, Highness. I am just the night shift. She's been asleep since I've been at my post." he pointed to a man in pale blue scrubs with a stethoscope slung around his neck. He had bags under his eyes, making his pale skin look even more sallow. "The doctor will know more."

"Thanks."

I left Jules' bed and made my way across the space to the man with the stethoscope. My bare feet made soft slapping sounds against the hard floor, betraying my approach. The doctor faced me and straightened as recognition dawned. "Your Highness, I wasn't expecting anyone so early."

"Couldn't sleep. Please tell me she's going to be okay. Has she said anything?"

"I'm afraid she's remained unconscious since we brought her in."

"But she should have woken up. She didn't hit her head."

He rubbed at the stubble on his chin. "We are still trying to determine the cause. Her vitals have improved somewhat, but she is running a low-grade fever."

None of it made a damn bit of sense. "Did you do x-rays or whatever to make sure she didn't break anything when the shield fell on her?"

He fixed me with a sympathetic expression. "We've run every test we can think of. We're still waiting on some cultures to come back, but we're monitoring her closely and we are doing everything we can."

"Is there any reason she wouldn't wake up?"

"Not that I can think of. Your Highness, I understand she is your friend, and you are worried for her well-being, but sitting vigil at her bedside isn't going to do anything."

"She's more than a friend ... like a sister. She's my family, you understand. So, do whatever it is you'd do if it were me or my mother laying in that bed."

"Of course."

Just then, the guard sitting at Jules' bed got to his feet, tugging the curtain back. I watched as Jules' eyes slowly fluttered open. Her pupils were wide and glassy. I pushed past the guard to be at her bedside. "Hey, you!" She licked her lips, but no words came when she tried to speak. I patted her right hand. "Just rest. You gave me quite the scare."

She swallowed—the act visibly painful as she grimaced—and croaked out, "Accident."

"I know, Jules. You just need to rest up. The doctors have you in good hands."

"Bow," she rasped.

"That's all in hand, too. We'll go on the next adventure together. Promise."

She tried to lift her right hand to reach for me when I noticed the bandage around her right arm was stained dark and a pungent smell wafted from it. Craning my neck, I called, "She's bleeding!"

All at once, a flurry of medical staff descended on Jules again and someone shoved me out of the space, yanking the curtains shut to give them privacy. The guard who'd been watching over her took me loosely by the bicep and guided me out of the medical area. A woman in a guard's uniform approached us.

"I need to fill my replacement in, Your Highness. Excuse me."

I couldn't stop him if I'd wanted to. My voice had abandoned me. All I could see when I shut my eyes was Jules laying in the bed, her wound bleeding profusely. I let out a shout of frustration and slammed my fist into the closest wall, the contact sending an ache reverberating through the delicate bones in my fingers.

Shaking the tendrils of pain away, I left the medical wing behind, allowing myself to wander in the silence of the castle. It did little to improve my mood and eventually, I found myself at the front doors that led into the courtyard. Throwing them open, I stepped into the cold winter air without a care that it was freezing outside. The sun had barely crested the horizon, and the sky overhead was still a deep purple. I could see smatterings of stars overhead and the moon was a sliver off in the distance. It was almost peaceful.

I settled on the steps, shivering as the thin fabric of my pants barely warded off the chill of the stone beneath me. I didn't bother with a jacket. I was too angry and part of me hoped the fire in my belly at the illogical array of Jules' symptoms would keep me warm. Time passed and the sky faded from that deep purple to a velvety blue and finally into a lighter shade. The moon and stars disappeared, replaced by the inviting light of the sun as it just kissed the tops of distant trees.

"There you are." Avery's voice pulled me from staring off at the world around me lost in my thoughts.

I looked absently at her for a moment, unsure why she'd be looking for me this early in the morning. She still wore the same clothes she'd been in yesterday when we'd convened our little research session in the library. A moment later, it hit me. She'd been working on some computer program to allow me to scan the Seelie castle.

"You hear about Jules?" The words came out almost robotic.

"I did. I'm sure she's going to be fine." She held out her hand to me, like she was going to pull me up.

But I wasn't ready to stand. When she made a grab-bing motion, I realized she wanted me to hand her something. "Give me your phone."

Slowly, I pulled it from my pocket and handed it over. She fiddled with it, tapping the screen, and holding her own device up to it, almost like she was air dropping something. I watched in fascination as she waved a hand over my phone, and I could feel a ripple of energy transfer from her outstretched fingers to the device. My magic recognized hers from our time fighting the Syndicate in Boston.

"This should allow you to map your surround-ings and transmit back to me in real time. I'll be able to convert the data into a digital model for the crown's records, for future use."

I took the phone back and spotted a new appli-cation. A tiny shield that looked like it could have been modeled after Camelot's coat of arms sat nestled between my phone's camera and contact list icons. It looked innocuous enough.

"Isn't that a little like spying though?" I asked, finally getting to my feet, and stepping back into the castle's warmth.

"They have three decades' worth of knowledge about the inner workings and layout of this place thanks to Arthur. I think it's time we got a little payback."

I eased the door shut behind me, letting out a soft sigh as the heat swept through me properly. I brushed bits of ice from my eyelashes as we walked side by side down the corridor towards the dining room. "You ought to get some sleep. Once Taron and I leave, we're going to need someone to monitor this in real time."

Avery barely stifled a yawn. "Yeah, but I need food first. Then sleep."

I didn't expect anything to be waiting for us and yet the table was laid out with plates, utensils, and mugs. From the smell, a fresh pot of coffee sat in the carafe at the center of the long table. Just as I sat down and poured myself a cup, my phone buzzed with an incoming text from Taron indicating they would be arriving in three hours. It was nearly showtime.

SIX

I was practically crawling out of my skin by the time the guards announced we had company at the front gates. I'd spent the last few hours flitting between the medical wing—being shooed away by exasperated nurses—and just roaming the halls. I was rubbish at waiting, especially when it involved people I cared about. Part of me hated the idea of leaving Jules behind, not knowing why her condition was so poor.

"The doctors seem really on it," Rory offered as we made our way down to the entrance hall. "And they've promised to keep you updated on any changes while we're gone."

"It was supposed to be her and me," I said before

realizing how it sounded. "Don't get me wrong, I'm glad I'll have you there with me. It's just ..."

"She's your best mate and you kind of thought this would be an adventure the two of you could do, together." Her tone was placating and sincere. And it made me want to scream.

I stopped walking and moved to bar her way forward. "You don't have to be nice, just because you think that's what's expected of you."

"I don't know what you're talking about."

"Agreeing with me, not being pissed that I basically said I'd rather do this with someone else."

"So what, you'd rather I called you a selfish bitch?"

"If it fits, yeah."

"But isn't that like treason?"

"I'd prefer it if the people around me were straight with me and called me on my shit."

"Okay, well then, you're being a selfish twat right now. You don't always get the things you want. I'll have your back because I know this whole mission is important and ultimately, we're connected by something bigger ... beyond finding the shield. But you're acting self-centered and insufferable." She tilted her chin upward, so our gazes met. "Happy?"

"Getting there."

"If you want, I can keep tabs on Julayne while you focus on the bow. We need you to be clear-headed after all."

"Don't hold back."

"You have my word." She stepped around me. "Come on, even I know it's rude to keep visiting dignitaries waiting."

I pivoted on my heel, and we made the rest of the short trek down to the entrance hall. Taron and Talia stood side by side, each flanked by a pair of armed guards. They wore deep purple and silver livery, and I noted the loose fit of the garments. No doubt they were designed for a quick shift from bipedal to four legs. Talia's hair was swept up into intricate twists encircling her head and helped secure a slender silver crown. Taron sported a slightly thicker version that settled on the edge of his hairline. His dark curls were pulled back into a knot at the nape of his neck. He wore dark loose-fitting pants and a long sleeve purple and silver coat with buttons that shone in the late morning sun coming in through the open doors.

He looked more regal than I'd ever seen him. I suddenly felt woefully underdressed. I caught Rory casting her gaze over his outfit, too. He gave me a quizzical look. "I had thought Julayne would accompany you."

"There was an accident. She's being treated in the medical wing. Rory's going to join us."

"Well, I do wish her a speedy recovery. It seems wholly unfortunate I haven't had the pleasure of her company."

For a moment, I was grateful Jules wasn't coming with me. I'd never hear the end of it, about where I was sneaking off to or where my mind was wandering with Taron so nearby. As it was, I anticipated similar commentary from Rory, if a bit more of the playful banter variety.

"Not to cut this short, but we'll be expected to arrive this afternoon for the start of the festivities. Before that we need to be sure what I've whipped up is going to withstand scrutiny," Talia interjected. She looked at the Camelot guards standing stoic at their posts. "And I suggest we do it somewhere that isn't so drafty ... or uh, visible."

"Follow me."

My mother's private sitting room was getting a lot of use the last few days, but she didn't seem to mind. I expected to find it vacant, but she and Emerys sat in deep discussion when I knocked and pushed open the door. Their conversation ceased the moment they spotted me which suggested I was the subject of their whispered words.

"Sorry to interrupt, but we need a private space to go over some things and I figured this was one of the most secure rooms in the castle."

"You don't need to explain. Please, come in," my mother answered and stood. She offered both Taron and Talia a respectful bow, which they returned with graceful dips. Emerys gave them a nod, but remained seated. My mother took a step closer to Taron. "You will be the one accompanying my daughter on this endeavor?"

"I am, Highness."

"She better come back to me in one piece."

"I would have it no other way."

She turned to face me. "Do you have any sort of plan for once you're actually there?"

I've got no fucking idea about a plan.

"It's safer if we keep the details close to the vest. Less chance of something slipping out."

She seemed to buy my bullshit as she fixed her gaze on Rory next. "I am trusting you to keep her safe, too, you know?"

"I know I'm no one in the grand scheme of the things, but I appreciate you putting your faith and expectation in me. I will bring her back no matter what happens."

"Do try not to incite a diplomatic incident," Emerys noted quietly. "We may be preparing for the eventuality of war, but that doesn't mean we are eager to be there."

"Talia's whipped up something that's going to ensure that doesn't happen," I said, putting the dragon princess on the spot.

Without missing a beat, Talia stepped forward and held out two simple pendants on braided silver chains. They twinkled in the ambient light, and I thought I caught a hint of pale blue or purple at the center. I took a breath and let my magic rise to the surface, feeling out the objects. My magic bumped against Talia and it made the pendants sparkle brighter. I'd have to remember to keep my power in check.

"These will mask the wearer completely from head to toe. To any outside observer, you'll appear as a full-blooded dragon. It will alter some of your physical characteristics as well as hide your magical signatures. For all intents and purposes, once you put these on, you're gone."

"Does it hurt?" Rory's voice was shaky as she tried to cover her nerves.

Talia cocked her head to one side. "You know, I'm honestly not sure. I didn't exactly have a lot of people to test it on."

"Then how can you be certain it will work as intended?" Emerys failed to hide the skepticism in her tone.

"Only one way to find out." I snatched one of the pendants from Talia's outstretched hand and slid it over my head, settling it against my skin next to the compass.

A wave of power washed over me as the spell took effect. It was like I'd stepped through the spray of a rushing waterfall and emerged a different person. I looked down at my bare arms and legs. They were a deep tan with a hint of olive complexion. My hair felt thicker and curlier. Running my fingers through the loose strands confirmed the texture had shifted with the rest of me.

"How do I look?"

"Beautiful, if not yourself," Taron answered with a sly grin.

I looked at Rory. "Didn't hurt a bit."

"Can you still use your magic?" My mother studied me with curiosity.

Doing simple magic likely wouldn't be an issue. Still, I pictured a tiny globe of light appearing overhead and, in a flash, it filled the space, burning bright and hot. But that wasn't what she meant, not really. I pressed my index finger to the sapphire on the bracelet encircling my left wrist. For a brief moment, my heart stopped, and air fled my lungs. The gem grew warm to the touch and the metal blazed against my skin.

Come on, it's still me.

The pain subsided and as I pulled my right hand away, Excalibur returned to its true form. My heart hammered against my breastbone as relief flooded me. To think I'd spent almost my whole life away from this blade and now the thought of not being able to access it, even for a short period terrified me.

"I wouldn't go waving that around," Talia noted. "Kind of a dead giveaway."

I took another beat to let the rush of emotion subside before sending Excalibur back into its hidden form. Turning back to Talia I asked, "Can I take it off if I'm alone or sleeping?"

"Technically, yes, but I wouldn't recommend it. You're going to be behind enemy lines. While the Seelie should give the royal retinue a wide berth, they know we're allies and could be keeping a close eye on you."

"Does this spell have a shelf life? Am I going to

turn into a pumpkin at midnight?" Talia and Taron gave me identical confused stares. "How long is the spell good for?"

"Ah, I see. It should last the duration of the festivities, but only just."

We had three days once we arrived to get what we were there for and escape before we no longer had the cover of Talia's magic. At least we knew that before going in. I pulled the pendant free and held it out to Talia. She took it and as she pulled her hand away, I watched as my skin lightened, and I felt like myself again.

"Right. So, now that we've got that taken care of, what's the plan?"

Talia cleared her throat. "I don't mean to be rude, but I think some plausible deniability is a good idea. I've done my part, and I'm going to return to our kingdom."

Without thinking, I pulled her into a fierce hug. She leaned into the gesture. "Do try to have a little fun amongst the daring deceit."

"I'll do my best."

"Oh, and you better behave yourself or you'll have me to deal with when this is all over." She made eye contact with Taron and for his part, I swear I saw him blush.

"I will not do anything to embarrass the Crown."

"Not what I meant, and you know it." She offered my mother another bow before passing the pendants to Taron and leaving the room. Emerys stood and gestured for my mother to join her. "I believe the Crown Princess has a valid point. The less we know the better as well."

My mother stood and approached me. "I know I have no right to dictate your life, but I am going to be very cross if you do not come home to me."

"I promise I'm not going to get stuck behind enemy lines or thrown in a dungeon. In and out before anyone's the wiser."

She leaned in and kissed my cheek. "Be safe."

I glanced at Emerys standing in the doorway. "You have any wise words you want to offer?"

"Uther is a ruthless and manipulative bastard. Do not trust anything he says or does. Assume nothing is without risk."

"Right."

She and my mother left the room, shutting the door behind them. Rory, Taron, and I were alone. I raked my fingers through my hair and rubbed my eyes. The lack of sleep and stress over Jules' condition were catching up with me, but I didn't have time to even think about rest. "We know what we're looking for. Once we find it, we're going to need to move fast."

"But we can't just walk out with it," Rory pointed out.

"We are going to need to leave something in its place," Taron noted.

I let out a hysterical laugh. "Sorry, that sounded like you said we need to forge an ancient magical weapon. So, that our greatest enemy is none the wiser to us stealing it."

"Well, I suppose that is one way of putting it."

I gestured toward him. "You aren't hiding forgery skills behind that sexy exterior, are you?"

"I may be a skilled craftsman, but no, I cannot fabricate Seelie magic."

"Let's think about this logically," Rory said, beginning to pace. "If it's sitting in his throne room, he's probably not using it. I mean, he isn't walking around shooting his enemies with it that we're aware of. He's probably keeping it under lock and key. Maybe we just need to make it look good, and not functional."

"Until shit hits the fan months or however long from now when he goes to use it and finds out it's a dud," I pointed out.

"But by then, he wouldn't have any reason to think it was us," Rory answered.

Taron frowned. "That's a big assumption."

I had half a mind to ask Jules about it before reality hit me again that she was in no condition to give me her thoughts on anything. We were going to have to wing it once we were in the castle. "Okay, assuming we're able to create a fake, is there any way we can sneak a bow in undetected?"

"Security is going to be stringent. No weapons permitted. Anything we need will have to be acquired there," Taron answered.

That didn't thrill me either. So much for this being an easy mission.

"Okay. Let's talk about how we're actually getting in. I didn't have a mirror, but I'm pretty damn sure I didn't look like your sister."

"Ah, yes. Well, you two will be posing as members of the royal guard. Given my status as a royal, I am permitted a small contingent."

"Won't the actual royal guards think it's strange?"

"I have vetted the real ones who will be accompanying us. They will not breathe a word of our plans or movements." The way his gaze narrowed as he said the word vetted suggested he'd done some additional interrogation of his soldiers to ensure they weren't hiding certain allegiances that could fuck us over. The Syndicate's head might have died in that cave in Ireland, but there was a reason the group had survived this long. Still, I appreciated his thoroughness.

"Okay, you're going to need to tell us everything we need to know in order for us to pass as your guards."

"Oh, I'm going to need to do more than tell you. We have a lot to do before we leave this afternoon. Let's get started." He smirked.

CHAPTER

SEVEN

Taron's existing protection detail were better sports than I would have expected as he dragged them into a back courtyard out of the view of prying eyes. The castle staff may have finally come to accept me as the next ruler of Camelot, but they still didn't need to be privy to our machinations.

"I didn't think we'd have to be brandishing weapons," Rory noted as the guard Taron paired her with adjusted the standard in her left hand.

"It's not a weapon," I corrected, pointing to the flag at the top. "We're announcing his entry, remember?"

"Oh, right."

"It needs to be higher," the man in front of me said, lifting my left arm up and bracing my elbow so I had the correct height. My shoulder and bicep muscles ached from the repeated practice. I also wasn't entirely sure the injuries I'd suffered in my challenge bout against Arthur months ago weren't being aggravated by the repetitive motion.

"We've been at this for an hour. There's got to be more important things for us to be doing other than holding flags," Rory complained, resting the end of the pole against the ground.

"You will not dishonor His Majesty with sloppy presentation," the guard, whose name I thought was Hagen, responded gruffly.

"I promise not to be offended," Taron said from the other side of the courtyard. "I'm also fairly certain these lovely ladies are capable of standing at attention without much trouble."

Expecting me to stand still for an undefined period of time was not a good idea. I hated being still. Besides, it didn't make the task any easier if I was confined to one place.

"You're sure we'll have a broader run of the castle this way?" I handed the pole off to the guard in front of me and approached Taron.

"Well, I suppose we could have disguised you as staff, but that seemed so unbecoming for a woman of your true station."

"If I'm being honest, I'd probably feel more at home that way. Almost easier, passing by without people giving me a second thought."

He slid a finger beneath my chin and tilted my face up until our gazes met. "I want you where I know you are safe."

"We could pass them off as trainees," Hagen suggested as Rory nearly dropped the pole when she handed it back to him.

"It is our hope that Uther will be far more focused on showing off his newly reunited heir to his own nobles and reassuring them that his claim to his own throne is not in question. Rather than him wondering why my guards aren't quite in sync on patrol," Taron answered.

I gave an involuntary shudder at the thought of Arthur being the center of attention once again. "Okay, so we've got the marching bit mostly down. I'm assuming we eat after you."

"Yes." Taron exchanged a glance with Hagen and his expression changed the lines around his mouth turning into a frown. "There is at least one ball during the festivities. And everyone invited is expected to attend."

My mouth went dry at the word ball. I wasn't a dancer by any stretch of the imagination. I was happier plying the liquor that inevitably found its way to turning the dance floor into a sticky mess than being in the spotlight.

"Can't I fake being ill?"

Taron shook his head. "That would only draw Uther's suspicions."

"Oh, come on, Morgan. Haven't you watched Strictly?" Rory said.

I rounded on her. "You're telling me you actually know how to ballroom dance?"

She shrugged. "Gran and I bonded over it. She got me lessons for my sixteenth birthday. I'm not a professional, but passable."

Taron stepped up to me and slid a hand down to my waist. "I suspected this might be the portion of our morning lessons that needed the most instruction."

"You better be a bloody miracle worker."

Out of the corner of my eye, I watched Hagen offer Rory his hand, his irritation at our sloppiness fading as she flashed him a confident grin. Taron snapped the fingers of his free hand and music began playing around us. It was a soothing, simple melody. I could even pick out the steady beat with its one-two-three lilting cadence.

"You are lucky. You just have to follow," Taron said as he began guiding me around the courtyard in a triangle pattern.

"Trust me, I think it's safer for everyone if I just stay standing on the sidelines," I protested as I stumbled, stepping on his toes at least twice as I spoke.

He didn't seem to mind. Though, for all I knew he'd shifted the skin on his feet into scales for protection. The music changed, picking up tempo and turning into a livelier rhythm. I watched Rory as she adapted to the change without losing a step.

"I am not going to let you fall," Taron said in my ear as the music changed yet again, turning into something that felt far more sensual. His hand tightened on my hip, and he leaned me back.

"You're enjoying this," I quipped as I watched his gaze travel the length of my neck and to my exposed chest. A flirtatious smile graced his lips as he pulled me out of the dip.

"I enjoy every interaction with you, Princess."

He snapped again and the music stopped. It was only then that I realized the music had emanated from the second guard's mobile phone. I had to hand it to him, he was quite an adept DJ. Rory's cheeks were flushed as she offered Hagen a curtsy. He returned it with a bow before straightening and turning to address Taron. "I trust Princess Talia provided us with the necessary items to disguise your allies?"

"My sister is nothing if not thorough. We should have everything we require."

I glanced around the courtyard. If Talia had packed anything, it was ingeniously hidden, because I saw nothing resembling luggage for any of us. "Clearly I'm missing something," I said, making a sweeping gesture around the space. I also didn't recall seeing them come in with anything when they'd first arrived either.

Taron made a 'hand it over' gesture to the other guard—I really ought to remember his name—who tossed him a slender drawstring bag I hadn't noticed during our training session. Taron undid the tie and opened the bag to show me the contents. I took the pouch from him and slid a hand into the opening, feeling layers of fabric. My fingertips brushed against what felt like tough leather boots with metallic clasps. I withdrew my hand and turned the bag over in my hand. "Remind me to ask her how she did this."

"Some magic is best kept a secret," Taron noted.

"That means he's got no idea how she did it," Rory quipped with a smile.

"I do not question my sister's gifts, of which there are many. Come, you two need to change. We will need to depart shortly."

I passed the bag back to Taron and waited as he extracted our guard uniforms and boots. At least the clothing was meant to be loose. I slung the fabric over my left arm and said "Meet you at the back exit in twenty minutes. We don't need people seeing all of us leaving together."

"You ought to send an escort, so we don't get lost," Taron suggested. "It isn't polite to have nobility wandering aimlessly through the halls."

"Oh, right." I felt momentarily foolish for not realizing the difficulty of Taron making his way through the castle like he owned it. Or for assuming he'd know where to go.

I retrieved my phone and sent a text to Gethin. He wouldn't be pleased to play dragon babysitter, but I knew he'd be discreet and understood the sensitivity of what we were about to do. With that done, I led Rory back inside and up to my bedroom.

After all these months, it was finally starting to feel like mine. I handed over one set of trousers with a top to Rory as I stripped down to my underwear.

"Do you think you should leave that here?" Rory pointed to the bracelet on my left wrist.

Instinctively I pressed my finger to the tiny sapphire and the object shifted into its true form. No doubt everyone in the Seelie castle knew what Excalibur looked like. After all, it had only been encased in stone for three decades. Merely the blink of an eye for a Seelie. It would be a dead giveaway I wasn't just some dragon guard. But the thought of leaving it behind made me physically ill. As far as I knew, no one in Uther's court knew that I'd had it transfigured. Even if the Seelie court were on high alert for spies, so long as I left it alone, it wouldn't give me away.

"No, it comes along. Besides, you never know when we'll need to fight our way out of a jam."

As I pulled on the loose-fitting top, a soft knock came at the door. I shared a look with Rory as we hurried into the trousers before I answered the door. Avery stood on the other side. Dark circles under her eyes told me just how little sleep she'd gotten in the last few days. "Good, you haven't left yet."

"Come to wish us luck?"

She shook her head and held out a small box across the threshold. "I realized that we needed a better way to communicate with each other while you're undercover. I doubt you can walk around with a Bluetooth headset the whole time."

I opened the box to find two simple diamond earrings nestled against a soft white velvet cushion. "I'm guessing this isn't just pretty jewelry."

Avery gave a tired smile. "Thanks to a little help from Emerys, we turned them into a communication device. You just have to tap the stones once to disengage, otherwise they'll transmit, and we can hear whatever you do."

"Brilliant." I hooked a thumb at Rory. "Got a pair for her, too?"

Avery's cheeks flushed. "I didn't really have time for one pair."

"It's okay. It's not like we're going to be separated much," Rory said, lacing up her boots. The boots molded to fit her feet precisely.

I pocketed the jewelry and gave Avery a hug. "Thanks for this."

"I wasn't going to let you walk into enemy territory without backup. Besides, it's not like you're going to have the tools at your disposal for research while you're there. You're going to need help."

"Just try to rest, too, yeah? You won't be any good to me if you're exhausted."

She took off her glasses and rubbed her eyes. "A few hours' sleep isn't a bad idea."

"Come on, we need to meet them," Rory urged.

I sat on the edge of the bed and tugged on the boots Taron had given me. Maybe they were magic too, because the moment I laced them up they fit as if they'd been made just for me. I plaited my hair to keep it out of my face and followed Rory down to the first floor. We wound our way along the back corridors to the exit where we found Taron, Gethin, and the two guards waiting for us. For his part, Gethin didn't look overly perturbed I'd asked him to be their guide.

"Avery gave you the earrings, right?" He stepped forward to meet me as we approached.

I patted my pocket. "We're ready to go."

"Not quite." Taron held up the pendants Talia had crafted. "It doesn't do to have the Crown Princess be seen leaving in our company when others certainly know our destination."

I took the one he held out to me and studied it. I couldn't deny that my nerves were starting to get the better of me. There were so many ways this could go wrong and the consequences for all of them were disastrous. Yet I couldn't back out. The compass had sent me on this mission for a reason and I needed to see it through.

"Please come home to us, Morgan. We did just get you back," Gethin said, pulling me into a fierce embrace.

"Taron has already promised my mother I'll return in one piece. And at the first sign of trouble, we'll abort and just come home."

"I'm holding you to that." He moved on to Rory, giving her a hug. I noticed she held the embrace tight.

Securing the necklace's clasp behind my neck, I felt the magic wash over me. My hands rippled in front of me as my skin darkened and I could feel the subtle shift of my facial features shift. My legs ached briefly as I grew taller. Beside me, Rory donned her pendant and underwent the same changes. Her hair was the most noticeable as the red vanished, replaced by a deep auburn. Her eyes took on a slightly deeper hue as well.

"So, what now?" I turned to Taron and felt my brow furrow. The voice that had come out of my mouth was not my own. It sounded like a mixture of accents blended together. It wasn't unpleasant, but it was going to take a lot to get used to it. Hopefully,

Avery had taken this into account so she would know her earrings hadn't been stolen.

"Whoa, this is weird." Rory held a hand up to her mouth, equally surprised by the change in her voice, too.

"We should depart," Hagen said, pivoting on his heel toward the door behind him.

"Yeah, about that ... how exactly are we meant to get there?" I did my best not to fiddle with the bracelet on my wrist. "You promised no shifting."

"We can't be seen arriving by portal," Hagen noted.

"And we won't." Taron looked at me. "And you will not need to shift forms. We can fly you there and land at such a distance that we can return to human form and approach on foot."

My anxiety ebbed a little at his words. "We can do that."

"I hope you are not fearful of heights," Hagen gave Rory a wink as he offered her his arm.

"Love 'em." She glanced back at me and mouthed, 'This is amazing.'

I followed Taron out into the cold air, shivering as a gust of wind blew through me. I regretted not trying to find a way to wear layers under the uniform to help keep me warm. Taron wrapped an arm around my shoulders, and I felt warmth ripple from his body. "Are you ready to infiltrate the enemy?"

"Ready as I'll ever be."

Time to go steal a priceless Seelie relic right from under Uther's nose.

Taron led our group of five a good distance away from Camelot's castle before he gave the order for the guards to shift form. I averted my gaze as they did so. I might be comfortable watching Taron make this transition from man to beast, but I didn't know Hagen or his companion. They deserved privacy to make the switch. Rory followed suit, going so far as to copy me and turn her back entirely. I waited until I heard loud snuffles from behind me. I turned to see two coppery dragons standing before us. They offered Taron a bow and he returned it, bending at the waist. He gathered their clothing and boots, stowing them in the bag before beginning to disrobe himself.

"You know, you'd think after however many

centuries you all have existed someone would come up with a way to allow you to keep your clothes," I said.

"You would think so, and yet, not a single person has bothered," Taron answered cheerfully as he held out the bag. "You'll need to hold to this until we land."

I scooped up his clothes and stowed them before securing the bag through one of the unused belt loops on my trousers. I reached out and gave Taron's snout a pat before approaching his outstretched talons.

"Uh, what are we supposed to do now?" Rory called.

"Climb in between his talons and hold on tight. Oh, and unless you want your eyes to freeze, I'd keep them shut."

She gestured skyward. "It's freezing out here. Aren't we going to catch our death?"

"Just trust me. They wouldn't do this if we weren't going to make it there."

Her unfamiliar features betrayed her fear as she marched up to the dragon standing tall behind Taron. I hadn't fully paid attention to whether it was Hagen or his companion, but it didn't matter. Either one would get her across the border. Checking the bag at my waist one last time, I settled into Taron's large talons. He closed them around me, placing me close to his chest before his wings beat in the frigid air around us. In a smooth motion, he launched himself into the air, moving with more aerodynamic grace than anything his size had any right to. The heat generated from his breathing held back the tiny icicles already fighting to form on my eyelashes and strands of hair that hung around my face. I nestled as close as I could to keep that warmth around me. I forced myself to keep my eyes open long enough to see the castle grow smaller as we rose higher. Taron banked to his right and gave me enough of a view of our traveling companions to see Rory similarly tucked up close to her dragon companion's chest.

Despite having been in Camelot for months now, I still had a terrible sense of distance. I knew Taron could cover a decent amount of ground in his dragon form, but the time needed to cross into Seelie territory was still an unknown duration. As we continued through the air, I shut my eyes. Being this high up meant that any details I could discern would be distorted and wouldn't do me any good in tracking where we were heading or where we'd been.

It felt as though we traveled for hours. Taron and

his guards flew on and I occasionally opened my eyes, raising a chilled hand to brush ice crystals out of my vision. My legs, while warm, grew cramped and stiff the longer we stayed in the air. Oh, how I longed to have done this trip via a portal. It would have been so much faster and less ache-inducing.

'You don't know where you're going.'

The voice in my head sounded an awful like Jules.

Well, she was right. I'd never set foot in Seelie territory, let alone anywhere close to their castle. I couldn't portal to somewhere I'd never been. And so, I shifted position to try and relieve the discomfort in my lower extremities as Taron banked right again and the sun struck my face. It was warm given our height and I relished its glow. When we finally began our descent, I forced myself to open my eyes. I might not know where we were about to land, but I could do my best to commit it to memory in case we ever had a reason to visit again.

Please don't give me a reason to come back.

The ground came at us faster than I'd have liked. Instinct took over and I braced myself against the scales rippling over Taron's chest. Thankfully, he didn't balk at the sudden change. Instead, he nestled me closer, blowing out a huff of air that sent heat cascading over me and I sighed. The grass below us was a brilliant shade of green even though it was definitely almost evening. The sun overhead was cresting toward the horizon. Yet even as our escorts' bodies cast shadows over the ground, it was still lush and luminous. It was fascinating and I found myself trying to sense what sort of magic might be keeping it so vibrant in the winter. My power bumped up against Talia's spell again and it struggled to find purchase.

Come on now, none of this.

Lime tickled the back of my throat, and I could make out something shimmering just above the grass as Taron landed. I couldn't tell who'd cast the spell or when, but I could see it thriving despite the elements. I had to give it to the Seelie, they could make some really fucking pretty things. Taron set me on my feet before taking an ambling step backwards. I caught the outline of his shadow distort and change as I opened the bag, rummaging for the clothes he and his men had discarded in Camelot.

"Okay, that was kind of terrifying. But also, really cool," Rory explained, teeth chattering intermittently.

"How much time did we lose?" I handed Taron his trousers and shirt before moving on to Hagen and his friend. They waited to begin their transformation until I'd set the clothing down and turned my back. I focused on Taron as he settled his shirt into place, looking regal as always. He reached for the bag, and I undid the tie, passing it over. He stuck his hand inside for a moment, retrieving his crown from the depths. Placing it on his head he secured it in place.

"Are you ready?"

"Don't have much choice." I spread my arms out to my sides, trying to encompass our surroundings. "Where are we exactly?"

"About a twenty-minute walk to the Seelie palace grounds," Taron replied as he produced four standards and poles from the bag. It really was a bloody useful bit of magic. "We'll have to walk from here. No flying that close to the grounds."

I let Hagen arrange Rory and I into the back corners of the square as we marched in formation around Taron through the fields. In short order, we reached a paved road, and I spotted brightly colored flags hanging from trees and power lines overhead. Everything felt warmer here, too. As if the cold of winter was being kept at bay by nature herself. If I didn't know any better, I would say we'd walked through yet another portal into a different reality altogether. I couldn't deny it was alluring.

The Seelie deal in deadly beauty, I reminded myself. I had to be on high alert now that we weren't within the safety of Camelot's borders. I turned my attention to the road in front of us. I could hear the cacophony of voices ahead as we reached a long queue of vividly dressed people with pale complexions and obviously pointed ears waiting to gain entry.

The grounds just outside the castle walls were as lush as the field we'd landed in earlier. Except they were dotted with delicate purple and pink flowers. Rory bent to study one before Hagen caught the motion and stomped his foot. "Do not touch. They're deadly."

"Sorry," Rory murmured and stood back up, resituating her grip on the pole in her hand.

"I wouldn't trust anything here to not try to kill you," I whispered.

"Then it's going to be a long couple of days if we aren't going to eat or drink anything."

"Oh, Uther doesn't want that sort of publicity. He's not going to poison his guests," Taron replied. "Start a few fights, now that could be deemed nightly entertainment. He was one of the biggest proponents of bringing the annual tournament of champions back."

My mind flashed to my first introduction to Camelot and the world in which I was supposed to have grown up. I didn't have to look far to find Uther's brutal influences in the event. Pushing that from my mind, I focused on trying to blend in as we passed through the gateway. Taron produced an invitation from his pocket, and I watched in silence as he handed it to a slender Seelie guard checking in guests.

"No Crown Princess?" the guard questioned, giving Taron a wary glance.

"She was indisposed. You'll have to settle for me and my friends here."

"Four guards for one man?" one of the guests sneered. His nose was so angular and pointed he literally had no choice but to look down it at us.

"Can't be too careful when royalty heirs seem to go missing with alarming regularity around here," Taron answered before giving a small flick of his wrist that the guards in the front of our formation understood to mean 'keep going.' And so, we left the entryway behind. We passed through an opulently decorated courtyard with marble statues that appeared to glow from within and into a receiving hall. There were more people milling about in the space than I expected. Apparently, we'd arrived just as everyone else had and the festivities weren't underway yet.

"You can set those down for a minute. We'll be formally announced and then you don't have to bother with them again," Taron explained quietly.

I set mine against a nearby wall and as I shifted my weight, I felt my phone in my pocket. Avery's mapping application still needed to be activated. Sensing I needed the cover, Rory moved to block me as I retrieved the device and double tapped the application. It opened, showing a bright green square with a check mark, and then returned me to the phone's home screen. Now wherever we went, Avery would know.

Just as I'd stowed the phone back in my pocket, the inner doors opened. Hagen and his companion fell back into step beside Taron. Rory and I took up the rear and waited as others within the hall filtered inside. I craned my neck, trying to see where we were going. Only we were toward the back and too many Seelie nobles blocked my view.

"Prince Taron," a deep male voice boomed.

We marched into the room, finally giving me a view of the inside. Uther sat on a tall black velvet throne beside a woman who looked vaguely like Arthur. The offending offspring stood off to Uther's right. A young woman with pale hair and bright blue eyes flanked the Queen. Taron offered a deep bow when we reached the front of the room. I watched Hagen to see if we were required to bow or not. Thankfully, he didn't move.

"The realm of fire and air are honored by your invitation, King Uther," Taron said, his voice carrying not a hint of distaste for his surroundings or the man he addressed.

"We do hope you find your time enjoyable," the queen answered in an airy tone. "Festivities will begin in earnest in the morning. Food will be brought to your quarters this evening."

"I look forward to the next few days." Taron rose and pivoted on his heel, leading the way out of the room.

THE DOOR CLOSED BEHIND ME. I found Taron standing at the window, staring out at the night sky. I hesitated to call it a beautiful view since we were still behind enemy lines; but I couldn't deny that everything did look lusher and more vibrant here. I tapped the earrings in my earlobes once to cut the communication feed.

"You wanted to see me?" I asked, pulling his focus from the window.

He turned at the sound of my voice and closed the distance between us in a few broad steps. "I did."

"Was it something important? It's late and if any of the castle staff saw me sneak into your room, they might start spreading rumors."

He laughed. "You think I pay attention to Seelie rumors about who I take to my bed?"

"Well, your girlfriend might get jealous," I quipped, faltering on the label. We hadn't really defined things. Besides, having sex a few times didn't exactly mean we were in a relationship.

"Hmm, there is that." He reached out, cupping the nape of my neck and undid the clasp of the pendant Talia had given me.

The moment the metal broke contact with my skin, I felt a sudden rush of power ripple over my body. My tanned skin had now returned to its normal coloring. I could feel the connection to my own magic, which had been severely tamped down, spring to attention. Excalibur, which I'd taken to concealing in my pocket, warmed as it, too, found our connection restored.

"What are you doing?" I hissed, making a grab for the pendant. "Someone could come in."

He tossed the pendant on a nearby chair and waved his hand at the door. I heard a click as the lock engaged. "No one is going to disturb us. And besides, I wanted to kiss you." His hands reclaimed their position at the nape of my neck. "The real you."

I didn't fight him as his lips found mine. I'd grown used to the heat his body gave off and leaned into its familiarity and comfort. It felt right to be with him. The kiss lasted only a few moments, but I savored every bit of it.

"I wish everyone could know you as I do," he said with a sigh when he finally broke the kiss.

"I'm not much for sleeping around," I retorted.

"Not what I meant, and you know it." He pulled me with him as he sat on the edge of the bed. I landed in his lap. "I only meant that you are unlike any royal I have ever met."

"That's because until seven months ago, I didn't really believe I was one. And my Aunt Nim didn't raise me to be one."

"And that is precisely what makes you so different and in a good way. I'm starting to think you are precisely what this realm needs right now; a fresh perspective."

"You really do know how to butter a girl up," I said, looping my arms around his neck.

"I wasn't aware I needed to," he said, falling backward against the bed and bringing me with him.

I cast one last glance toward the door before I let myself get lost in just being with the man I was absolutely falling in love with. For just one night, I'd forget about the danger lurking beyond this room and just let myself be loved.

CHAPTER
NINE

I woke early in the unfamiliar surroundings. Taron slept soundly beside me; arm thrown over his head as if he didn't have a care in the world. At least waking up beside him was a familiar feeling. I slid from beneath the sheets in search of my clothes, tugging on the guard's uniform as quietly as I could. In the mirror, I did my best to tame my hair back into a respectable plait. I didn't know who I might run into in the corridors when I left and needed to maintain my cover.

Now that I thought about it, this early in the morning wouldn't be a bad time for a little reconnaissance. Maybe I could even map the whole of the main level. I was halfway to the door when I realized I'd left the pendant where Taron had discarded it the night before. I picked it up and secured the chain around my neck. My mouth went a little dry as I watched the transformation in the mirror. The spell came over me like a wave, rippling from head to toe. My features distorted into the mask of my dragon counterpart in an instant. Turning back to Taron, part of me wanted to wake him if only to tell him I was leaving. But he knew I had a mission to complete.

Our night together was a lovely distraction, but it was time to focus. Stepping into the corridor, I glanced in both directions before I tapped the earrings once. "Anyone there?"

"Do you have any idea what time it is?" Avery's voice came through loud and clear in my ear.

"Uh, no actually. Left my phone in the room."

"You've been silent for hours."

"Well, that's generally what happens at night-time. People sleep."

"You turned off the feed."

"You lot didn't need to hear me snoring all night."

"Right. Snoring," Avery said with a hint of joviality.

"Look, I'm sorry if I worried you, but I'm fine. Nothing's happened. We were served food in our rooms last night and all the festivities are set to start today."

"Five o'clock," Gethin's voice filtered through the earrings.

"What?"

"That's what time it is."

"Oh, cheers." After a beat, I added, "Hang on, did the pair of you get any sleep last night?"

"We took shifts. Look, now might be a good time to start mapping things out."

"My thoughts exactly. Once I get my phone." Except that meant I needed to figure out where Rory and my room was again. It had been a brief walk last night, but now it seemed a bit hazy. I closed my eyes, trying to retrace my steps. I turned left and walked past three identical doors before one opened and a semi-familiar face appeared and yanked me inside.

"Avery's been blowing up your phone for hours."

I gestured to the earrings. "She's already scolded me. I've just come to get my phone and set out to see what I can find."

"You shouldn't go alone. Besides, it looks less suspicious if we're together."

"She's not wrong," Avery's voice echoed in my

ear. "Besides, you need someone to watch your back."

I caught Rory's mouth working as if she wanted to say something, but she held her tongue. I retrieved my phone, cleared the numerous missed calls and texts from the home screen, and opened the mapping app. To my surprise a tiny diagram took up a portion of the screen. From what I could tell, it had mapped the path from the receiving hall to the guest quarters one floor up.

"Let's go."

While knowing the layout of the guest quarters didn't seem the most important use of our time, I led the way along the corridor, trying to gauge who resided within each. Rory gave me a curious look when we stopped long enough to let a twig-thin Seelie woman with a long purple plait down to her waist exit her room and make her way down the nearest staircase.

"If we're going to be doing what we came to do, it's better to know if we're surrounded by enemies on all sides," I said in a whisper.

"Maybe Avery can do a little facial recognition to give us a sense of who all these people are."

"Probably easier to do in a crowd. Less conspicuous," I said as we moved down the corridor and hit a dead end.

We pivoted and made our way back past our own room and Taron's. I glanced at the closed door, momentarily picturing the prince laid out beneath the sheets. We made it to the next door when it opened, and Hagen appeared looking bright-eyed and rested.

"You two look like you're up to something."

"Just getting a lay of the land to make sure the prince is safe," I answered.

"You've been here before, right?" Rory cozied up to him. "Anything we should watch out for?"

Hagen gave a deep throated laugh. "Everything with pointy ears. They'll act all proper and posh to your face, but they'd stab you in the back the moment you look away. Trust nothing you see or hear."

"Come on, we'd better see what's down the other end before we head downstairs." I tugged Rory away from him as we made our way along the remainder of the corridor.

"I can't decide if he's just trying to be overly cautious or if he really thinks all Seelies are manipulative, cutthroat bastards," I said under my breath, hoping Avery or Gethin would hear.

"Just because you got to grow up with the only Seelie who apparently fought her own nature and was a decent person, doesn't mean everyone's had that experience, Morgan," Gethin noted. "We're not proud of the divisions in our world. But they still exist and breaking that distrust isn't something that happens overnight."

"I get it. Bigotry is everywhere."

We found a second staircase at the other end of the floor and made our way to ground level. My phone gave a little happy chirp. I pulled it from my pocket long enough to see a little notification that we'd successfully mapped one area of the castle. My heart beat a little faster as we left the relative quiet of the guest quarters behind and entered the already bustling lower floors.

Despite the early hour, the castle staff were darting in and out of view, carrying large trays of food and drinks. Apparently, Uther intended to feed his guests into submission. I spotted the purple-haired woman lounging by one of the open windows, a glass of what looked like champagne in her hand.

"Bit early for a drink," Rory murmured as she too caught sight of the woman.

"It's five o'clock somewhere," I retorted. "Come

on, let's see if we can find the throne room and get a proper look at the bow while no one else is around."

We slipped through a partially open doorway that led to a short corridor and a set of ornate silver gilded doors with multi-pointed stars for handles. My hand shook as I pushed the doors open and peered inside. Tall portraits lined the walls as the daylight illuminated the faces. They all looked haughty and judgmental, and a bit like Uther and Arthur. But there was no hint of thrones or other wall decorations in sight. It was too much to hope we'd simply stumble upon our desired destination on the first try.

"You think one of these blokes is the one who got the bow in the first place?" Rory asked as we eased the doors shut.

"Probably." I couldn't quite understand the purpose of the room. It housed no furniture where people could sit and admire the art. It just seemed odd to have a space that wasn't practical.

We retraced our steps to the hall where the staff were laying out breakfast and my stomach burbled with hunger. I'd been too nervous to eat dinner the night before. Truth be told, I'd been a little fearful they'd somehow figured out who I was and attempted to poison me.

"We need to keep looking," Rory urged.

"I know. But I'm starving." I watched as the purple-haired woman set down her glass on a nearby table and it miraculously refilled itself. A server came by with a plate of what appeared to be scones and she plucked one from the tray before shooing the server away.

"I wonder why she's up so bloody early," I said as the server came our way.

"Maybe she just doesn't like to sleep. Or she wants the good scones before they disappear," Rory answered.

I didn't trust that the nobility here wouldn't try to murder me if they found out who I was, but this woman intrigued me. I couldn't quite explain why, but I was drawn to her. And so, after picking up a scone of my own, I marched over to her.

"Morning." I pointed to her champagne. "Mind if I ask where you got that?"

She pivoted to look at me and I was surprised by the softness in her features. When she spoke, her voice was the pitch of tiny tinkling bells. "One of the delightful servers snuck it up for me. I could see about getting you some, if you'd like?"

"Oh, I'm not much for bubbly this early in the day."

"You may find you change your mind by tomorrow."

"You don't sound like you're too pleased to be here."

She gave an exaggerated sigh. "My family was supposed to send my older brother. But he had the indecency to come down with some made up malady and I had to come in his stead. I had plans. The King isn't the only one throwing parties to celebrate the Solstice time."

"So, you're preparing yourself to put on a smile and pretend to have fun?" Rory interjected.

"Precisely." She tilted her head to one side. "You're in the dragon's livery."

"We're new recruits," I blurted. "The prince thought it would a be a nice simple assignment to accompany him to get our feet wet."

"I'm afraid I've never had the pleasure of his company. I've heard he's a bit reclusive these days."

"Oh, he's got plenty of things to keep him busy." I failed to hide the defensive note in my voice.

"Well, I'm glad he was able to grace us with his presence, even if he likely did it out of political allegiance to Camelot." She ground out the last word through gritted teeth.

"You know, given this is our first time attending

one of King Uther's festivities, it would really go a long way to impressing the prince if we knew what to expect."

The woman gave another dramatic sigh. "Now, I haven't been to one of these celebrations in ages. But from what I remember, today there'll be lots of mingling in the morning. The afternoon has lots of games and then tonight is a banquet. Tomorrow is the big show though. Uther is specifically honoring Arthur's return home. That's why so many of the nobles turned up."

Having all the focus on Arthur might, for once, be to my advantage. If the Seelie were all zeroed in on him, then maybe we could slip in without being noticed, nick the bow, and get out. I took a bite of scone, and my stomach dropped as a thought hit me.

"Just so we're prepared in case things get out of hand, where is this big celebration for Arthur happening?"

"Throne room of course. Apparently, there's some big ceremony to properly name him as Crown Prince."

Damn it.

"Thank you again for your help, uh ..."

"Lady Luanna," she said as I turned to leave. "And you two would be?"

My mouth went dry again and this time it had nothing to do with the magic that had transformed me into a stranger. We'd completely forgotten to pick names. Rory could get away with using her real name. But the moment I let my name slip, we were fucked.

"I'm Rory and this is ... Tracy," Rory filled in, not losing a step.

"Curious names," Luanna said.

"Enjoy your breakfast," I blurted before dragging Rory away. "That was close."

"Probably should have sorted that out earlier."

"At least we have an idea of where everyone's going to be today. We could do our best to slip out unnoticed while everyone else is busy."

"You two should really figure out where the throne room is before it gets much busier." Gethin's voice came through the communication device in my ear, jarring me with the unexpected commentary.

When I glanced back over my shoulder, Luanna had drifted off, possibly chasing after a server for another scone. We'd lost her attention for the time being. Trying to look like I knew where I was going, I left the space, and this time turned left down the corridor that connected to the receiving hall at the front of the castle. The sun was already above the tree line on the horizon and the light bounced off the pale stonework, momentarily blinding me. I blinked the spots from my vision and felt a hand on mine. Rory dragged me forward and pointed to another ornately decorated door, this one inlaid with gold, rubies, and black stones that could have been obsidian.

I tried the handle, opening it inward on silent hinges. I managed to peek inside long enough to spot the bow on the wall. I started to move into the room to get a better look at how it was secured to the wall and assess if there was any magic protecting it when Rory hauled me out and shut the door.

"Someone's coming."

I stiffened as I picked up on the sound of rhythmic foot falls against the stone flooring. There was still a chance we could sneak back to breakfast without being noticed. Except I realized the foot-steps were coming from the direction we'd traveled, which meant whoever it was had already seen us and we'd have to pass them on the way.

Trying to look official, I stood tall and fell into

step beside Rory as we walked back the way we'd come. A young woman approached us carrying a tall stack of linen, balanced precariously in her arms. Her foot caught on a crack in the floor and the fabric fell from her arms, covering the stone between us.

"Oh, fuck me," she muttered.

"Here let me help you with that," I offered.

I bent to help her, and our gazes met. My heart stopped the moment I had the chance to fully take in her face.

Aunt Nim?

But that was impossible. I'd watched her die in our flat back in London. And this woman was so much younger than Nim had ever been. But I couldn't deny she was the spitting image of the woman who'd raised me and given her life to save mine on more than one occasion.

So, who the hell was this woman?

TEN

The other woman recovered her composure first as she waved a hand, and the linens reassembled themselves in her arms. She stood with her gaze averted as if she realized I was supposed to be someone with station.

"Please don't tell anyone I did that," she said, not looking me in the eye.

"Did what?"

"The King hates it when staff are ... vulgar."

I let out a snort in spite of myself. "Oh, his precious ears never heard a curse word before?"

That got her attention. Her head whipped up and our gazes met. Hers narrowed as she studied me with curiosity. "You should not speak ill of your host."

"Don't listen to her. She's just cranky before she's had her morning coffee," Rory jumped in.

The woman nodded the way she'd come. "Food is being served in there."

"Right. We were just getting a lay of the land as it were. Can't be too careful when you're protecting royalty," I said.

She cocked her head to the right in a contemplative gesture I'd seen Aunt Nim do a thousand times in my childhood. "Something tells me that you aren't really looking out for your liege. But I won't say anything if you keep my little secret."

"Deal." I held out a hand to shake hers, forcing her to rebalance the linens for a third time. "I'm Emma. This is Rory. And you are?"

I caught Rory giving me a dirty look at the sudden name change, but she kept silent. I waited, hand outstretched for the woman to take it and answer my question. Finally, she gave it a quick squeeze and said, "Saoirse."

"See you around," I said as she hurried off in the direction of the throne room.

Rory waited for a beat before rounding on me. "Why'd you change it up?"

I shrugged. "Felt more like an Emma." After a breath, I added, "And I sort of panicked."

"I noticed. Mind telling me what that was all about?"

"Not out in the open. Come on, we should go check on Taron anyway."

"You mean you didn't check on him before slinking out this morning?"

"I didn't slink," I quipped as I led the way upstairs. "Besides, there's nothing preventing us from seeing each other."

I approached the door to his room and knocked much like I had the night before. I waited and watched as the handle turned. Taron appeared in a deep blue silk shirt and dark grey trousers that evoked Camelot's colors.

"You left without saying anything," he said, opening the door wide enough for us to enter.

"I didn't want to wake you. Besides, we did a little scouting of the castle."

"Right. You want to tell me why you freaked out over a servant?" Rory gave me a pointed look.

"She was the spitting image of my Aunt Nim."

"Maybe just being in this place brought up memories of her, given that she had to have spent time here if Uther gave her the mission he did," Taron suggested.

I shook my head, the plait bouncing against my

shoulders. "She looked exactly like her and sounded like her, too." I pivoted to look at Rory. "That head tilt she did ... God, Nim did that to me as a kid all the damn time."

"Younger sister, maybe?"

"She never mentioned family to me at all."

"If she fled with you on the day of your birth, it is conceivable she believed any relations she still had would be hunted down and punished for her betrayal." Taron sounded so matter of fact as he spoke. "Don't act so surprised. Uther nearly forced a woman to murder an innocent newborn. Casual acts of murder to set an example doesn't seem far from what he's capable of."

He wasn't wrong. Though if she was somehow related to Nim, I needed to talk to her. She should know that Nim was actually dead and had saved my life.

'Be careful, child.'

Nim's voice echoed in my mind the moment the thoughts occurred to me. Confronting Saoirse would blow my cover in an instant. And simply because Nim had been kind and loving to me, didn't guarantee any of her relations would feel the same way. Still, I couldn't shake the feeling that I'd met her for a reason.

"Did your early morning snooping yield anything else of interest?" Taron diverted the conversation.

"We met a Seelie noblewoman who's about as fond of Uther as we are," Rory answered. "And we found a creepy room just full of portraits of past rulers."

"I saw the bow in the throne room. But that's when we ran into Saoirse. We need to get back down there. According to Luanna, there's going to be mingling this morning and games in the afternoon. I'm guessing that Hagen could handle your security detail during that."

"Yes, I would suspect he can, although he may not like it."

"Come on, Uther's not stupid enough to do anything to you just because you've only got two guards with you instead of four."

Taron offered me a smile. "He is concerned with your safety, too, Morgan. In fact, I would wager he is far more concerned about protecting you than me."

"But I'm not a damsel in need of protecting."

"No, you're just a princess in disguise, intending to steal a relic from a foreign power who actively hates you. I gave your mother my word I would return you home unharmed and my men take that pledge seriously, too. I think it safer if you allow Hagen to accompany you."

I caught Rory offer a small pout at being split up —or maybe it was because she didn't get to enjoy Hagen's company—before she brightened again. "I'm pretty good at small talk and smooshing. Gran says I'm a natural party person."

"Then it seems your talents are far better served with me. How about we go make our presence known?"

Taron stepped into the corridor and Hagen materialized seemingly from thin air at his side. "Highness. Are you ready to go down?"

"Rory and Solomon will be joining me. You'll be accompanying ... "He glanced at me to fill in the blank.

"Emma."

"You and Emma will be completing some ... private matters for the crown."

"Understood," Hagen said.

Solomon appeared next to Taron and fell immediately into step with the prince. Rory hurried to match him, and they marched down the corridor towards the stairs closest to Luanna's quarters. I turned to Hagen. "I don't think I said thank you for letting us do this."

"High—Emma, I do not do this for you. I do this for my prince. He has found your cause worthy and whether you know it or not, he has pledged himself to it. That means I have as well."

"You make it sound so ... formal."

"We dragons do not do things informally. I was led to believe you have crossed paths with several of our kind since your return to Camelot."

"One who spent eight hundred years in the world where I grew up protecting a priceless treasure and another guy hell bent on eradicating all other races. Not sure both extremes are a great sample size."

"No, I suppose not." After a moment, he gestured for me to take the lead. "Tell me where we are headed."

"Throne room." I paused and looked at him. "How much did Taron tell you about what we're doing?"

"The broad strokes. And unless absolutely necessary, my only request of you is that myself and Solomon not be brought into the details."

"Plausible deniability. That's fair."

"Sometimes I forget just how short-lived your kind are. No doubt if Uther were to find out we had anything to do with your caper, his memory would be long and vivid. He would make us suffer long after you were dead."

"Cheery thought."

"Yet, an honest one."

"Okay, well how about this? I just need you to keep look-out for me and distract anyone that comes by. Nothing illegal or overly dangerous."

"I can do that."

As we descended the stairs, I picked up on more voices filling the space below. Little clusters of people spilled out of the dining hall and their conversations mixed into unintelligible white noise in the background. I was grateful that no one seemed to pay us any mind as we went about our business. I walked as purposely as I could toward the throne room, hoping that anyone who did stop us would see we were just patrolling the area. Hagen for his part kept stride with me, matching me step for step. That sort of synchronized movement must have been drilled into him from his guard training.

"Can I ask how long you've been in the Dragon Guard?" If we were going to be spending even a little time together it would serve me well to know more about the dragon.

"Since I turned twenty. It was an honor to be chosen."

"Oh, it's not something you apply for?"

"It is something one trains for with the aspiration that you are selected. The crown must be careful."

"Syndicate spies."

"Precisely."

"Did you know about Taron's interest in the subject?"

"In truth, I have spent most of my time assigned to the Crown Princess, ever since Prince Taron stepped down and passed his claim to her."

"She's pretty badass."

Hagen smiled and his eyes lit up. "That she is. I am in no rush for our ruling monarch to step aside. But when her day does come, she is going to bring about sweeping change for the better."

"Sounds like my kind of ruler." I just hoped I'd be around to see it happen. Being Camelot's queen didn't seem so bad or daunting if I had Talia at my side as an ally.

As we moved down the corridor towards the ornate door that led to the throne room, I scanned the space, trying to see if I could spot anything like hidden cameras or other magical traps meant to deter trespassers. Nothing stood out and that put me on high alert. I didn't believe for a second that

Uther would leave his throne room unguarded. The fact I couldn't see anything obvious just meant I had to determine what sort of cunning danger lay in wait.

"I would suggest whatever you must do, you do it quickly. I may be skilled in many things, but oration and verbal distraction aren't chief among them," Hagen said.

Now he tells me.

"Give me five minutes."

He turned and blocked the view of anyone coming from the direction we'd just travelled. I focused on the doorknob, reaching for my own magic to try and sense anything that might be lying beneath the surface that my previous visit hadn't picked up. Nothing was obvious, at least not on this door anyway. Swallowing the lump in my throat, I eased the heavy door inward just enough to squeeze through. I scanned the vast space for something to use as a door stop, but couldn't find anything. I said a silent prayer that it wouldn't lock me inside and crept through the space. The thrones here were similar to the ones I'd seen the night before except these had thin veins of silver threaded throughout the velvet crisscrossing into almost constellation patterns.

I stopped myself short of running a finger over the fabric as I passed. Why was everything in this place designed to be so damn eye catching? I approached the bow mounted to the wall and my heart sank. I could already make out the bow was secured with thick metal braces to the stonework. They looked like they'd been welded in place and situated, so that one would need to snip the bowstring to get the rest of it off.

Up close, the bow was sleek and shone in the ambient light. It was beautiful and sent shivers dancing down my spine at the thought of the damage it could wreak on me and the people I cared about. I reached a hand out toward the weapon and my fingers immediately began to ache, as if they'd come too close to a fire. Shaking my hand out to dispel the pain I took a step back. Either it sensed who I really was or even those it perceived to be dragons weren't going to lay hands on it. Clever bastards.

Closing my eyes, I summoned my magic, biting down on my lower lip until the taste of blood mixed with the sharp citrus of my power. I sent my request out into the world that I needed to see the spells keeping the bow protected. When I opened my eyes again, I could see tiny strands of magic covering the bow like a spider had come along and made its home there. I could see several strengthened anchor points at the center and ends of the bow. The braces shimmered an eerie purple beneath the webbing and when I moved my left hand closer, it rippled, shifting from a dark purple to a violent shade of violet. My wrist throbbed as if caught in a vice grip. It was all I could do not to cry out in pain. I could almost feel the magic fueling Talia's spell in the pendant waver.

Backing away as quickly as I could manage, I let the magic drop. The wispy bits of magic faded slowly from my vision with each blink. The pain in my arm receded even slower still. I cradled my hand to my chest, as if I'd suffered a physical injury as I retreated to the doorway. I tried it, but the door wouldn't budge.

Oh, fuck.

With my right hand, I knocked three times. I held my breath, waiting in silence for Hagen to get the message and open the bloody door. Each second that ticked by was agony. Finally, the door opened, and he stuck his head in. "We need to leave. The royal family is on the way. We can't be seen here."

Wordlessly, I followed him out of the space and cast about for an exit. I needed to put distance between myself and the magic in that room. Somehow, Hagen understood my need. He clamped a hand on my right elbow and steered me to an archway. I hadn't noticed it before, but we emerged into an open-air garden filled with swaying yellow flowers. White marble benches dotted the space and I sunk onto the nearest one. I flexed my left hand and wrist again, relieved to find the pain had mostly gone.

"I trust your visit was illuminating."

"Not sure I'd say that. I've got no fucking idea how we're supposed to make this work."

"Something tells me you aren't going to just give up because the task at hand has become complicated."

I caught sight of Luanna passing by the interior corridor and a thought flashed through my mind. I didn't have a reason to trust her, but she just might prove useful. Time to make friends with the Seelie nobility.

CHAPTER

ELEVEN

Hagen and I made our way back towards the dining hall in search of Taron and Rory. As we walked, the bright sunlight from outside struck the pale stonework around us and my vision blurred. My body swayed and I put my hand out to steady myself. I felt Hagen's firm hand on my back as he guided me to a small alcove and forced me into a seated position.

"Tell me what is wrong."

"I—I don't know." I blinked again, but the blurriness refused to subside. My hand tingled again, and I bit back a sudden wave of nausea as a thought struck me. What if the magic protecting the bow had somehow recognized me as the sworn enemy of the Seelie royals and was slowly working to dismantle the magic keeping me hidden? I looked down at my hands, I could swear the pigment shifted a few shades closer to my natural tone.

"Look at me."

I forced myself to meet the guard's gaze and my vision cleared. I felt something like heat ripple across my hand where he pressed his fingers to it. When all of this started, I never would have imagined dragons could be such skilled healers. Taking another steadying breath, I tried to get to my feet.

"If you need a message passed to the prince, let me relay it."

I shook my head. "What I must ask of him should come from me. I'll be all right."

Hagen glanced over his shoulder and back to me with frown lines tugging at his lips. "I'm not sure you're cut out for whatever you have planned. I mean no disrespect, but you do not look well."

I tugged my uniform into place and stood tall. "I'm fine. I was just letting Uther get in my head. The bow is protected by Seelie magic. We should have anticipated that. We just need a way to get around it and I think I've got one."

"Mind filling us in on your plan?" Avery's voice filtered through my earrings.

"Let's just say we're going to get someone whose

magic won't be seen as a threat to bypass the security."

"You mean someone Seelie?" Gethin's voice chimed in.

"That's the plan."

"Good luck with that," he muttered. After a moment, he added. "I just mean you aren't exactly going to find many people who would defy their own king inside his castle to help you."

"And that's where Taron comes in."

Taking the lead again, I marched towards the hall and pulled open the large doors. I scanned the crowd and finally found Taron next to some men with sharply pointed ears. I turned to check the other side of the room and spotted Luanna standing slightly apart from the rest of the crowd, glass in hand. Looking as official as I could, I walked over to Taron.

"Excuse me," I said, resisting the urge to tug on his arm to get his attention.

"You let your staff speak to you like that?" one of the men, with a bald spot covering the crown of his head scoffed.

"We enjoy a more familiar repartee with those in our employ," Taron answered and turned his back. "I trust everything is as it should be?"

"There is a small matter that needs your attention."

Taron gestured for me to lead on, and I wound my way closer to where Luanna stood. Taron fell into step beside me, and I clocked Rory flanking us through the crowd. She was taking her playacting seriously. "You look a little pale." Taron's words made my heart skip a beat and I found myself subconsciously touching the pendant around my neck.

"I found the bow, but it's protected by Seelie magic. I'm guessing we're going to need someone with Seelie power to bypass it. Otherwise, we'd need to take out an entire section of wall and something tells me Uther would notice if we blew up his throne room."

"That would certainly lack subtlety, yes."

"I met someone earlier who might be convinced to be sympathetic to our cause ... Lady Luanna."

"She has a reputation of being something of a party girl."

"The fact she's been downing champagne since six o'clock this morning would certainly add to that assessment. But she was also taken with you."

"And you want to use that natural infatuation to our advantage."

In that moment I realized I hadn't taken into consideration whether he'd even want to go along with the plan I'd been concocting. I certainly couldn't force him to flirt with her and I didn't want to either. If I was being honest, I didn't love the idea of him paying that kind of attention to anyone else. But completing this mission was bigger than some petty pangs of jealousy over a possible relationship that had just barely begun.

"Morgan?" His voice was barely above a whisper in my ear.

"Yes, that's the plan. Don't tell her the whole plan, just try to get her to want to help you."

"I can do that."

I double tapped the earring on my right lobe. "And do try not to fall for her."

He smiled at me. "Seelies have many wiles, but I can assure you I am immune."

Rory crossed through the crowd to stand beside me as Taron made his approach. I tapped my earrings again to reestablish the connection with Avery back in Camelot. My stomach did a flip as Luanna's eyes locked on Taron drawing closer. She set her glass on a passing server's tray and fiddled with her hair. He offered her an elegant bow and held out his arm as he whispered something in her ear. Color turned her cheeks a vibrant shade of pink as she looped her arm through his and they disappeared from view.

"You hate this plan," Rory noted, her tone a deadpan.

"Really fucking do, but we need all the help we can get."

"Say she agrees, how are we supposed to get this thing out unseen?"

"The bag Talia gave us. It should be big enough to secret the real bow. And one of us can spell it to go unseen."

"That solves the how we get it out, but how do we make them think it's still sitting there?"

"Anyone happen to locate an armory anywhere? I know they've got magic, but my gut says Uther is still the type to use things like crossbows for fighting. It probably makes him feel superior."

"We haven't been able to find any accounts of where they might store weapons on our end," Avery answered.

I guess that meant we'd need to go snooping around again. I gave Rory's wrist a tug and nodded for her to follow me out of the hall. The corridor that led up to the guest quarters was empty and eerily silent. Not even our footsteps echoed in the space, and it set my nerves on edge. They should have made some amount of sound. Why would you muffle a potential attacker's approach?

"Would the compass be of any help?" Rory was walking backward to keep an eye on the way we'd come.

I felt foolish as I stopped walking. Of course it could help. The compass was meant to guide us on this damn quest. Surely, it had to know what we needed to succeed. I reached into my pocket and retrieved it. It sat cool and dormant in my palm as I studied the tiny etching on the silver surface. Summoning my magic to the surface, I put it out into the world with a silent request.

Help me find what we need to pull this off.

I waited for the compass to warm or illuminate a magical path through the castle. Instead, it simply sat in my hand not doing a damn thing. Had it not recognized my magic hidden under the layer of Talia's, like Excalibur had fought me at first? I tightened my grasp on the compass, but it remained cold and unavailing.

"Maybe it's confused?" Rory offered.

Or maybe it wasn't just my magic needed to get it jumpstarted. I grabbed Rory's hand and placed it over the top of the compass. "Give it a little push."

I felt her magic bump up against my hand and for a moment the compass grew brighter between our fingers. But it didn't point in a particular direction. If anything, it made the little hairs on the nape of my neck stand on end. Taking a slow breath, I pocketed the object and glanced over my shoulder. Nothing stood out, but that didn't mean anything.

"We're going to have to look for it the old-fashioned way." Blind luck.

So, we walked down the corridor without making a sound. We passed the room with the creepy Seelie portraits, and I felt a shiver dance down my spine. It urged me onward at a faster pace. We reached a set of descending steps, and I took the lead, throwing caution to the wind. If we happened upon any of the castle staff, we could plead ignorance of the grounds and insist we were in training. And yet, we found no one. Not even cleaning staff doing the washing or cooks preparing for what I was sure would be an elaborate meal for the banquet tonight.

"This feels off," I said to no one in particular.

"We can turn back."

Except that seemed like the wrong move. There had to be a reason the compass hadn't worked other than the dragon magic keeping our identities a secret. But I refused to believe it meant for us to abandon the mission. Besides, I'd been up against Seelie knights before, and I'd come out on top. Or at least I'd survived those encounters and that counted for something.

The hairs on the nape of my neck bristled again as we stopped at the foot of the stairs. A long corridor waited before us, that appeared to run perpendicular to the one we'd left above. Only it was darker here, although the walls were made of the same bright whitewashed stone. It looked more like what a castle was meant to be. The constant brightness and beauty above was unnerving. A series of unadorned wooden doors led off at varying points down the corridor. They had large metal latches and rings in the center rather than doorknobs. My stomach did a flip as I pictured this space being used to detain Seelie enemies. None of the doors had windows.

"You take the left, and I'll go right?" Rory suggested.

"Stay in the line of sight."

She gave an affirmative nod and moved down the corridor, leaving me standing alone. The fingers on my right hand flexed and I caught myself just before I'd touched the sapphire at the center of my bracelet. We might not have encountered anyone down here yet, but that didn't mean we were alone. So, I joined Rory in the search. The first door I tried was firmly locked. I looked ahead to see Rory standing in front of an open door and I skipped the two in front of me to join her.

It housed floor to ceiling shelves filled with crates of fresh produce and vegetables. Sacks of grain and cornmeal sat on the bottom rows. I studied my friend's expression. She looked almost disappointed.

"They've got a castle of people to feed. It would be irresponsible not to have stocked up," I pointed out.

"I kind of thought they just did it all by magic."

"I'm pretty sure even they can't do that. Come on. We need to keep looking."

We resumed our search. As Rory eased the door closed. I thought I'd finally heard the sound of footfalls on the stairs. I froze in place, holding my breath as I listened intently. No one materialized and there was no shadow on the stairs from the light filtering down from above. Maybe I'd imagined it.

Moving back towards the stairs, I tried the two doors I'd bypassed. One opened to reveal a similar layout to the one Rory had discovered, except this one had linens. The third was also locked. The majority of the others were similarly laid out with dishware and table settings.

"We aren't going to find what we need here," I told Rory.

She'd stopped to stare at a blank stretch of wall. From where I stood it looked unremarkable. However, when I moved to stand beside her, I noticed that the stones had a strange, discolored pattern.

"Are you thinking what I'm thinking?" Rory's voice was quiet, conspiratorial.

"That Uther is too much of a perfectionist to allow this sort of color variation to go unaddressed."

"Unless it's done on purpose to conceal something else."

"Like an armory?"

"Maybe."

"Can you take a picture of it?" Avery's voice made me jump.

I took my phone out and snapped a photo, sending it off to her. I took a step closer to the wall and held up my right hand, palm flat. I could feel power emanating from the stonework. It was definitely magically protected. Though with my luck it could only be opened by a Seelie. Somehow, I doubted even Taron could convince Luanna to come down into the bowels of the castle to be alone.

"If we had more time, I'd say see if you could dust for fingerprints. Maybe we could come up with a pattern on the stones," Avery said.

But we didn't have the time. And neither of us had anything to dust for fingerprints. We weren't the police. Just then my pocket grew warm, and I plucked the compass out. It was a bright purplish color, and the stones suddenly lit up like a blacklight had shone on them. I heard Rory's sharp intake of breath at the sudden assist. I took a step closer and the compass' light flared. One of the stones grew brighter than the rest.

"Give that one a go."

Rory pressed her hand to the stone, and I heard it click as it retracted into the wall. Another discol-ored stone three down and two to the right bright-ened next, followed by one in the center, and a fourth on the very bottom left. She pressed them in sequence, and I heard a more pneumatic hiss as the wall fully retracted and darkness dropped off in front of us. I held the compass aloft to cast some light to reveal yet more winding stairs. Oh, joy.

I stepped onto the top step and unseen sconces

flared to life, lighting the way. I made it down a few more steps before Rory moved to follow me.

"Stay up here in case things go sideways."

She moved to block the way, bracing her arms on either side of the opening. As I descended, my footsteps echoed in the tight space. Whatever magic had muffled us in the castle's upper levels was gone here. I just hoped I wasn't walking into a trap.

CHAPTER
TWELVE

I trailed my hand along the smooth stone wall as the stairs continued to descend on a curve. The sconces continued to offer patches of yellow-orange light ahead and behind me. How far down did this bloody thing go? I tried to peer into the murky darkness below me and my foot slipped on a bit of damp stone. I flailed, arms pinwheeling out to my sides as I fought to catch my balance. Someone finding me faceplanted at the bottom of this staircase was the last thing we needed. My right hand managed to catch a small depression in the mortar of the stonework and I kept from tumbling down. Heart hammering in my chest due to the sudden shot of adrenaline made it difficult to breathe and I could swear my vision started to go grey at the edges.

Get your shit together, Morgan.

"You still with me, Avery?" My voice echoed in the confined space.

"Yeah, though the signal is a little weaker than before. By the way the mapping app is still working."

At least if I got lost, maybe my friends would find me. Tamping down on my heart rate, I continued to follow the stairs deeper into the bowels of the castle; until I had to assume the path was subterranean. The air took on a slight musty, earth scent as I continued to walk. The farther I went, the more I believed that this wild goose chase wasn't leading me to an armory after all. The compass had not led me astray before, so I didn't have any reason to believe it would this time. And yet, unease wrapped around me like a heavy cloak. It made my movements sluggish, and my senses slow to respond. Finally, the shadows and the pools of light stopped disappearing just out of view. I had reached the end of the staircase.

I wiped cool sweat from my brow as I took in the dark, uninviting surroundings. This space was clearly not kept up to the same standards of the halls and guest quarters we'd left behind. As long as the shiny veneer distracted visitors, it didn't matter what happened behind the scenes. But it looked about right for what I knew of the majority of Seelies, especially the nobility. Moving away from the foot of the stairs, the light cast by the sconces dissipated, as if the atmosphere behind it sucked up the light by magic. For all I knew, that's exactly what was happening.

I wasn't about to go any farther blind. I held out a hand and in my mind's eye, I conjured a sphere of bright green light, miming tossing a ball skyward. Lime tickled my taste buds as the spell coalesced overhead. I held my breath as I took a few tentative steps into the darkness. My heart slowed for a moment as the light faltered and sputtered before stabilizing. With the orb of light dancing along overhead, I left the relative safety of the only way back to civilization and marched into the unknown.

I moved forward in what felt like the direction I'd been going when Rory and I had been checking the doors overhead. And yet logically that seemed impossible as we'd reached the end of the corridor. Then again, given how far below ground I assumed I was presently, it wasn't beyond the realm of possibility that Uther had built tunnels that snaked beyond the castle.

I plucked the compass from my pocket again and

held it aloft, praying it would give me a clue. It gave off pale wisps of blue light and seemed to tug back toward the way I'd come. But that made no damn sense. Nothing was behind me save for the staircase and Rory at the top keeping watch. Neither of us had an alternate bow to use to fake out Uther or anything else to put our plan into motion. In that moment, as I stood in a barren, musty corridor, reality hit me in a tidal wave. We only had a day and a half left to get a proper plan in order and make our move.

That sense of panic was enough to make my heart skip a few beats. I'd faced worse odds before, I reminded myself. Even getting into the tournament six months ago had been a slim chance. Yet I'd managed it. I could pull this off, too. I refused to go back empty handed, regardless of the promises I'd made to my mother and Emerys. Pushing forward, I finally came to another set of unassuming wooden doors with their large round handles. These doors, unlike the ones on the floor above, sported small metal latches that appeared to slide from side to side. Like ... prison cells.

My stomach did an undignified flip as I moved my hand to spread the light out to illuminate more than just my immediate surroundings. The greenish glow rippled over the dull metallic rings on seven or eight more doors. Well, fuck.

Glancing down at the compass, I realized it was starting to grow brighter. The bluish hue mixed with the green overhead to give off almost an aquatic feel. The light danced across the stone masonry around me. It made my stomach lurch as if I'd suddenly stepped onto a boat in choppy seas. Out of the corner of my eye, I spotted something like movement. A shadow danced across the light around me, and I whirled around. I hadn't heard anyone approach and yet the sense that I was no longer alone struck me. Right before something hard smacked me upside the head. Stars flared in my vision as I staggered sideways into the wall.

"Morgan?" Avery's voice was full of concern and sounded miles away.

My eyes tried to focus on the spot the attack had originated from, but all I could make out was a blurry shadow dancing just beyond the sphere of my magically conjured light source. I swung a hand out at the shadow, but met only open air. Still woozy from the surprise blitz, I staggered forward only to feel something crack against the base of my skull this time. Blood filled my mouth as I bit down on reflex and crumpled to my knees. Swallowing turned out to be a really bad idea, as the thick blood only served to make me gag right before the light overhead blinked out of existence, casting me into darkness.

SOMETHING violently bright danced along the edges of my eyelids, rousing me. I groaned and winced when I felt the bite marks in my tongue. It didn't feel as though I'd completely bitten through it at least. It still didn't make the pain any less irritating or the injury less awkward. I managed to open my mouth and spit out a pool of blood. I tried to move my hand to wipe my mouth only to realize I was restrained. The brightness persisted and I forced myself to open my eyes one at a time to find a torch shining in my face. The kind the police used back home in London.

"What the fuck?" I said, my voice thick due to my swollen tongue and the ache in my head.

"You didn't think you'd get away with this, did you?" The speaker, decidedly female and somehow familiar, stood on the other end of the light. It was impossible for me to make a visual identification.

"I don't know what—" I began, but my captor cut me off.

"You come into this kingdom pretending to be something you're not. You're just as arrogant as you sounded in that interview."

Interview?

What was she talking about? I shifted my weight, trying to make the throbbing in the base of my skull ease up. Wait, I recalled the disastrous interview I'd done before everything went off the rails and I got pulled into this bloody quest. But that had never aired. My mother had made certain of it.

"That never went live. The Queen quashed it."

My captor let out a harsh bark of disbelieving laughter. She shifted the light enough to reveal an enlarged image projected onto the wall beside me. I craned my neck to see it playing bits of the interview. "The king is very persuasive, and people are willing to do anything if it benefits them in some way. With a bit of well-timed magic, it could be broadcast in real time to anyone. In this case, the king."

"And you," I noted. My head ached as the image faded and the harsh light returned. "Who are you?" I blinked rapidly, trying to clear my vision, but it was no use. The damned light just kept blinding me. "Look, I'm no threat to you. Cut the bullshit and at least let me see who's accusing me."

Mercifully, the light faded, and a face swam into my field of vision. My heart stopped. For a split second, I was looking at the woman who'd raised me. The nurturer, the Seelie who'd spared an innocent baby's life and done what she could to prepare me for the destiny that lay ahead.

"You're the girl with the linens," I blurted.

"And you're a usurping bitch."

None of this made sense. How could she have possibly figured out who I was? I'd only been without Talia's spell while I was in Taron's room, and I'd watched him cast protections on the room before we'd spent the night together. There was no way she could have any clue who I truly was. Unless ...

Awkwardly, I tried to feel for the pendant around my neck. But my skin was bare. In front of me, she held up the pendant, looking haughty. "I'll hand it to you; this was a halfway decent disguise. If I hadn't seen the prince before, I'd have assumed the lot of you were frauds."

"You're Nim's daughter," I said, hoping that Avery or Gethin would pop into my ear and tell me someone was on their way to find me and make this nightmare end.

"Figured that out, have you?"

I nodded slowly so as not to aggravate the headache thrumming along inside my skull. "You look just like her. Your name's ..."

"Saoirse. Is that supposed to make me feel better?" She stuffed the pendant in her pocket and hefted the torch by the handle as if readying to swing it at me. "You are nothing but a manipulator."

"You think this is my fault?" I sat up as best I could with my arms chained to the wall behind me. "I was a newborn. I had no say in what happened to me. I get Uther probably fed you some bullshit story, but he told her to kill me all because he wanted power."

"She left me."

I shook my head and instantly regretted the gesture. "No. I know Nim. If she had any choice in the matter, she'd have taken us both."

"Oh, right, you said she was such a loving, doting maternal figure in your life."

"Am I sorry she raised me? Not for a second. But you must see that Uther is the one manipulating you. He could have let you believe you were an orphan. But he made sure you knew who your mother was and what she'd done, at least in his twisted version of things. Why is that?"

"So, I would know my place. I have had to live with the shame my entire life."

"He wanted you to hate her for what she'd done. But it's clear you crave that relationship with your mum. Believe me, I missed out on a childhood with my mother, too. Someone stole that from me. I get your anger, because I feel it, too."

"Do you blame the prince for what he had?"

"Honestly, sometimes I do. But I am trying really fucking hard to remember that he was an innocent at the start of all this. Uther is the one moving us all around like bloody pieces in some elaborate chess game. So, be pissed at him for ruining all of our lives."

"But he's, my King."

"He's a conniving bastard who uses children as bargaining chips."

"I should turn you in right now."

I gestured as best I could to our dim surroundings. "Yet you've got me locked in a dungeon. Before you do whatever you're going to, just tell me one thing. How'd you figure it out?"

"Saw you snooping around the throne room. You and that other dragon guard. I've seen him before and figured you'd wormed your way into his security detail somehow. And I could see the residue on your hand."

"What residue?"

"You tried to undo the magic in the throne room. Magic always leaves a trail if you know what to look for."

I flexed my left hand on instinct. Maybe I should have been more careful and put up an invisibility spell to hide our wanderings. If she'd caught wind of what I'd been up to, it was possible Uther knew, too. Then again, the fact she hadn't turned me over yet suggested he was oblivious.

"I'd say I'm usually better prepared for things like this, but that'd be a lie. I just sort of get thrown into these situations and it's always the people I've got around me that help me get out of them."

"I could kill you." The threat was accompanied by a large knife she produced from somewhere on her belt.

"Yeah, but I've got people who know I'm here and they'd notice if I didn't come home. And they'd have a pretty good idea of who to blame for it. I'm pretty sure you don't want to start a war any more than I do."

"Why are you after the king's bow?"

"Honestly, I'm not really sure."

"You're not a very good thief if you can't even admit why you're stealing something."

"That's because it doesn't come naturally to me. I'm a bartender by trade. All this royal and political shitstorm stuff is foreign to me. I know the universe sent me here for it and there's got to be a reason for it, even if I can't see it just yet."

"What, you just get messages from the universe?" she sneered.

In the back of my mind, I could hear a voice that sounded a lot like Emerys warning me not to trust this woman. And yet, I felt drawn to her. Maybe it was because she was Aunt Nim's daughter, but it felt as though I was meant to share this with her.

"I had a compass when you knocked me out. It was glowing. It only does that when it's pointing me toward something that I'm going to need to complete one of these quests. But I don't understand why it was leading me down here."

Saoirse held up the compass and it nearly blinded me like the torch had done. "Does it usually glow this bright?"

"Only when I'm right on top of whatever it wants me to find."

She tilted her head to one side and studied the object in her hand and I was reminded of Aunt Nim when she was trying to puzzle a particularly confusing crossword puzzle clue. "Has this 'whatever' ever been a person?"

I thought back to my trek down here and the moments the compass had signaled that what I was after was close. It had been trying to guide me back towards the stairs ... because she'd been following me. She was somehow the key to completing this whole quest.

THIRTEEN

I'd hoped the revelation that the compass meant for Saoirse to be part of this plan would have encouraged her to release me from my chains. Instead, she studied the object in her hand, her eyes reflecting the ever-brightening blue glow. It was as if she'd forgotten I was even there. Her pupils constricted to pinpoints and the ambient light washed out her already pale skin as she fell into what I could only classify as a trance. I wanted to know what she was seeing and a small part of me was jealous she was getting some sort of communication from the compass. It had always been *mine*.

Struggling against the chains around my wrists, I awkwardly used my legs to push myself up the wall until I could at least feel the ground beneath my boots. I swayed a little as the change in elevation made my head swim. After a deep breath, the dizziness faded, and Saoirse still stood transfixed by the object. Testing the restraints, I found that at this angle I could reach out about four or five inches in front of me before the chains cut off my forward momentum. Just close enough to get a hand around the compass.

I didn't expect the jolt that zapped me, dancing along the tiny nerves in my palm and fingers. They twitched and danced, locking my hand in a vice around the object and Saoirse's hand. I tried to free myself, but it was as though we'd been cemented together. Her gaze never wavered from the light that now shone through our interlocked fingers. Something like a hot flash cascaded over my body and the tiny dungeon cell vanished.

All at once, I was standing on a grassy embankment that sloped gracefully down the edge of a river. It wasn't a place I recognized, and yet it still held a sense of familiarity. The sky overhead was an alluring mix of early morning purple, orange, and pink. I could just make out the barest hints of blue at the far edges of the horizon. There wasn't a cloud in the sky and the air tasted sweet on my tongue. I did a slow turn and found two female figures standing farther down river. I approached and they both looked up. They could have been carbon copies of one another, save for the broad grin that adorned the woman's face who stood closer to the water.

"There you are," Aunt Nim called, opening her arms for an embrace.

Saoirse stood beside her, looking aggrieved by the fact that I'd gotten such a reception. I wasn't about to forego the embrace of the woman who'd raised me simply because it annoyed her daughter. I knew this was all from the workings of magic—likely the universe trying to find a way to bind Saoirse and I together—but I leaned into my Aunt Nim's torso, smelling the sweet scent of her shampoo.

"This is how it should have been," she said softly as she let me go and turned to Saoirse. "Know that I never wanted to leave you."

"So, she said."

"I was no one before the king summoned me into his throne room and demanded I do his bidding. I didn't even know he knew I existed. And yet, not long after your birth, I was called to the castle for an audience. He ordered me to secret myself in Camelot's castle and when the time came, I was to take the newborn heir and ... dispatch the child."

"There wasn't anyone you could have left me with? No one who could have met you on your way out of

Camelot?" Saoirse's question carried a little less venom than her earlier statement.

"Oh, child, I was alone in this world. Your father never knew of your existence and even if he had, I fear he would have been no safer a place for you than the confines of the castle. And even if I had wanted to leave you in the care of a trusted friend, Uther gave me no choice. You were snatched from my arms. He told me he would kill you if I failed to comply with his edict."

"Yet I'm still here and you're the one who's dead."

"She was murdered by Uther's soldiers," I countered.

Aunt Nim held up a hand and Saoirse closed her mouth. I followed suit and waited for her to speak again. "The moment I held Morgan in my arms, I knew I could not do as he'd asked. No child deserved such a fate. But I also knew once news got back to him that I had failed, he would stop at nothing to kill her. So, I ran. I fled this realm to a place where I prayed the babe would be safe. But before I left, I cast a spell of my own, one I hoped would take root and grow as time passed. I begged the world's power to keep you safe." She reached her hand out and stroked Saoirse's cheek. "And it has. You may hate me for the choices I made, but do not let that pain and grief cloud your heart. I refuse to believe he molded you in his image. No child of mine was born to be cruel or vindictive."

"But ... you chose another woman's child over your own," Saoirse repeated.

"In a perfect world, I would have chosen both of you. I would have raised you together. Not a day went by, I did not think of you and hope you survived. There were so many nights I had laid awake, contemplating ways to sneak back through the barrier and bring you home with me. But it would have been too dangerous for all of us."

"We can't change the past, no matter how much we want to. What's important now is that we find a way to move forward together, because on every single one of these quests, it's been just as much about the thing I'm looking for as the person I'm meant to find it with. Whether we like it or not, that seems to be you. I'm not going home empty handed. So, you can either help me, or you are going to have to kill me and my friends, sparking an international incident."

"I'm not a killer," Saoirse finally responded. "But I'm not saying I trust you. You've been my people's enemy my entire life."

"That is not true," Aunt Nim corrected. "Uther may have given you a version of the truth, but he is not foolish enough to spread such rumors throughout his kingdom. Not before he was ready to control the narrative."

"If I had never showed up, no one would have ever been the wiser. Hell, I bet he had a plan to get Arthur *crowned Camelot's king and then work some political bullshit to ally with the Seelie."*

Saoirse's jaw worked as she chose her next words carefully. "He did restrict my movements once he'd told me the truth that you were out there. He made sure no one interacted with me outside of his or the queen's presence."

"They controlled everything about your life."

She shuddered and it shook her entire body. "I hate being used."

"I understand. And I swear to you, if I had a choice, I wouldn't ask you to help me. You have my word, when this is over, you're free to go wherever you want and do whatever you want."

Saoirse began to pace between Aunt Nim and I, her feet flattening out the blades of grass where she treaded. The water burbled in the background, and I still couldn't place our surroundings. The other two women looked far more at home. Was this some hidden patch of nature in the Seelie kingdom? It shared the same vibrancy of the castle and its immediate surroundings. Yet I didn't sense any threat of bodily harm lurking just beneath the surface.

"You two were meant to be bonded," Nim insisted again. "You have been given a chance to reclaim what

was taken from you; to stand against the tyrant who ripped both our families apart."

"Part of me wants to believe this is all just some fantasy, a bit of clever spell craft to lure me in ... and yet another part of me knows it is true," Saoirse murmured.

"I'll let you in on a little secret," I began. "I may be the lost heir and all that, but you've had thirty years to hone your magic. I've had six months with the full weight of my magic finally at my beck and call. I don't have the skill to weave something like this."

She smirked at me. "Now that I believe is entirely true."

"That is harsh," Aunt Nim chided.

"Nah, it's fair. She's not wrong. Look, help us and you get out of this hell. You get to be your own person. Please."

"I can't ignore what I've seen and heard here. And there is little chance that either of us would let the other walk free otherwise. Fine, I will help you."

Aunt Nim gave us a satisfied smile and wrapped us in a group hug before she, the placid river, and sunrise vanished. I blinked and my head ached at the sudden transition to the dark interior of the prison cell. My body slumped and if not for the chains keeping me erect, I'd have fallen flat on my arse.

When my vision cleared again, I watched Saoirse produce a small, brushed metal key from her pocket. She slid it into the manacle clamped around my right wrist and released the restraint. I shook my hand as she undid the other. A rush of power flooded me, almost like it had when I'd first tried to access my magic the day Emerys brought me through the portal.

I must have made a face because Saoirse said, "Magic suppressing restraints."

"Oh, right. Guess that's not just a Camelot thing."

"There may be a lot of animosity between our two peoples, but that doesn't mean we don't learn from each other."

"Or steal," I muttered.

The manacle around my left wrist clicked open and dropped to the floor and my arm felt as if it were on fire. The bracelet on my wrist flared a blinding white and without warning or any assistance form me, it shifted into sword form. We both stood there staring at the blade I now inadvertently brandished at her.

"I swear I didn't mean for that to happen. It's never done that before."

"That's Excalibur," she whispered.

"I see its reputation precedes it."

"I knew you'd pulled it from the stone, watched the bout broadcast, but I'd never seen it up close. It's ... beautiful."

Not the response I'd been expecting. "Uh, yeah, the dragons who made it did a bang-up job." I pressed my right index finger to the hilt, and it mercifully returned to its inert form. I hoped the sword's reaction was simply from being stifled and not a reaction to my latest frenemy.

"Here, you ought to put this back on." She passed over the pendant and I secured it around my neck. Talia's magic cascaded over me in a now-familiar wave and my features changed to match the face she'd designed for me. Next, Saoirse handed over the compass, which I pocketed.

"How long have we been gone?"

"An hour. Maybe more."

"Oh, fuck."

Frantically, I double tapped the earring on my right ear and a cacophony of voices came through all at once.

"Morgan? What is going on?" Avery's voice demanded.

"You need to find Taron. She's been missing for hours," Gethin added, though not directed at me.

"You need to trust that she knows what she is doing." Emerys sounded the calmest of the three.

"Uh, guys, sorry for the silent treatment. Things got a little ... complicated for a bit. But I'm okay. Things are fine."

"You can't just proclaim everything is fine when we haven't been able to reach you or Rory in hours. And none of you bothered to give us a way to get in touch with Taron or his guards." Gethin sounded as if I'd personally offended his whole family with my absence.

"Now that you mention it, that was probably an oversight." His comment about Rory was troubling though. He had her phone number and if my phone was still able to transmit the map, hers should have had a signal down here, too.

"Your accomplice was far too easy to subdue," Saoirse said casually as she led the way out of the cell.

"What did you do?" I demanded, not caring that my allies back home were likely very confused.

"I just incapacitated her. She'll be fine."

I sprinted through the darkness until I found the bottom of the winding staircase. The sconces had long since died out. Setting foot on the bottom step did nothing to bring them back to life. But it didn't matter. Blood rushed in my ears as I bolted upwards, flinging myself around the curves of the staircase until I finally made it to the top. Rory was nowhere to be seen.

My vision started to tunnel as I reached out for the nearest door, trying to pull it open only to find it locked. I spun at the sound of footsteps behind me to reveal Saoirse emerging from the hidden passage. The wall rejoined behind her, and she moved to the door directly across from me. She pressed her palm to the wood, and it opened with a soft hiss. Rory lay strewn against some extra bags of grain and rice in a secondary supply cupboard. I breathed a little easier when I saw her pendant was still in place. I knelt and shook her.

"Rory, come on. You've got to wake up, now, mate."

She gave a soft moan, and her eyes opened. They were bleary and unfocused for a moment. "Why does my head hurt?"

"Probably because you took a good whack to the skull. Come on, let's get you up."

"Who is she?" She gestured to Saoirse.

"A new friend. Let's find Taron and I'll explain."

Rory swayed as I got her to her feet and helped her out of the cupboard. Saoirse secured the door, and we walked slowly back through the corridor and up to the main floor. It was eerily quiet. I peered through the open doorway to our left and found a few staff cleaning up the remnants of breakfast and whatever else guests might have requested during the mingling session.

"They'll have moved out to the grounds for the games by now," Saoirse said.

That likely meant Taron as well. Hopefully, Hagen was with him, and no one was the wiser that the prince of a neighboring kingdom was plotting to steal from the Seelie crown. My stomach rumbled as I watched the remnants of food being swept into large barrels for disposal. I could have used a sandwich or one of Gethin's home-cooked multi-course meals, but food could wait. We were rapidly running out of time.

FOURTEEN

I made it all of a few steps in the direction I thought lead outside before Saoirse grabbed my arm and hauled me back the way we'd come. I tried to free my arm from her grip, but she held on tight.

"What are you doing?"

"You look a mess, the both of you. Besides, I'm guessing you've both got headaches that are making you see double."

"Not many people who beat you actually care about patching you up after," Rory said offhandedly.

"I'm trying to play nice," Saoirse retorted.

I wasn't going to say no if she had some magical cure all to make my head stop pounding. And I spotted bruising and chafed skin around my wrists from where the cuffs had rubbed my wrists almost raw. I didn't remember struggling against the restraints enough to cause that sort of damage. I studied my left arm and realized the injury was worse there. Maybe because Excalibur had been suppressed, too? Either way, if Saoirse had a way to alleviate the pain, I was all for it.

I tried to chart our path through the castle as she led us along side corridors I hadn't noticed during our first few passes on the main floor. I expected her to lead us down, but she ducked into a dimly lit passage behind a large wall hanging. The floor sloped upward until it let out one floor above. She moved with a quickness I assumed she'd learned as a member of the castle staff—get out of the way of the important people and don't be noticed—as she led Rory and I into a small room with a single bed and window overlooking a lush garden in full bloom. A floor to ceiling wardrobe sat beside the window and I could feel Saoirse's magic in the space. She must have spent a lot of time in here, experimenting with her power.

She finally relinquished her grip and in one fluid motion she sent me staggering to the edge of the bed. Rory joined me, resting her head on my shoulder, as if the whole thing made her exceedingly tired. I watched Saoirse open the wardrobe and rummage through some boxes near the bottom. When she stood, she held what looked like containers of dried herbs and other powders. In one hand she also held a dented cup. Moving to stand in front of the window, she emptied something from a clear bag into the cup. She swirled it so that the interior caught the sunlight filtering through the glass.

"So, what exactly were you planning to do?" She cast a glance my way before she returned her attention to her mixing. "You were clearly looking for something."

"I told you, we're after the bow. We don't know why exactly. I mean we know what we've read about it in our own records. It's immensely powerful and can target the wielder's enemies," I rambled.

"Never misses a shot. At least those are the stories that get told when the king's closest advisors get to drinking and reminisce about the old days," Saoirse confirmed.

"Anyway, that's what we're after. We were hoping we could find the armory, find an unadorned bow to replace it with."

"That's not going to fool anyone."

"We were going to make it look like the one we're taking," Rory interjected.

"Though, we didn't really have a good plan on

how we were going to do that. We just sort of figured we'd wing it."

Saoirse let out a laugh as she swirled the cup in her hand again before passing it to me. "Drink this."

I was about to ask 'drink what' when I looked at the contents. Either I'd been too out of it to notice she'd poured liquid in, or this was all fueled by magic. It was half full of a flowery scented concoction. I downed the liquid, and my insides turned oddly cool. My head grew heavy, and I felt myself starting to lean back in search of a comfortable resting spot. A moment later, my entire body was on fire, and I sat bolt upright. Sweat dripped from every pore, and I was certain I'd be sick. Slowly, second by agonizing second, the feeling subsided and when I could take a breath without my stomach threatening flips, I looked down to see the redness on my wrists had disappeared.

My headache had dissipated too and when I probed the two spots on my head where she'd struck me, they didn't hurt. In fact, I couldn't even tell she'd hit me at all. I passed the cup back and watched her repeat the process before handing it to Rory to drink. She grimaced as she downed it, and the cup fell to the floor with a loud clatter as her whole body went into convulsions.

"What the fuck is wrong with her?" I demanded, doing my best to get her onto her side and support her head.

"It'll pass."

Just when I thought Rory was about to black out, her body went still, and she let out a long rattling breath. "Ugh. That ... was gross."

"How's your head?" I asked in a gentle tone.

She blinked a few times before answering. "Better."

"Now that you two aren't going to arouse suspicion with the way you look, why in all that is blessed, would you think you could just replace an ancient artifact with a cheap knock-off?"

"Would you believe me if I said it works in the films?" I couldn't stop myself from laughing hysterically.

"Well, I thought it was a good plan," Rory mumbled.

"What you're proposing takes a lot more skill and preparation than you have clearly thought out," Saoirse critiqued.

"I'm open to suggestions," I replied.

She set the cup and leftover herbs back into the wardrobe and leaned against the wall. "The general idea isn't bad, exactly. Leaving something behind so they aren't aware they've been robbed, but this thing is a weapon of pride for the king. He will know if something happens to it."

"But you told me earlier he wasn't aware I'd been testing the magic keeping it secured to the wall."

"Because he's got to focus on all the people in his castle who aren't normally here. And this is the first time he's held any kind of celebration like this with Arthur back in his rightful place."

"We assumed we'd need Seelie help to get past the spells," I said.

"Actually, you're going to need more than just any Seelie's help. You're going to need mine."

"How's that then?"

"I don't know if he thought he was being clever or if he just assumed no one would ever notice me, but he purposely used me to cast the protection spell on the bow." She mimed pricking her finger. "He used blood magic. Only I can undo it."

Another hiccup of hysterical laughter slipped out. "Oh, this is brilliant. He's underestimated his enemies and he's going to get fucked over by his own hubris."

"He never thought you'd be important," Rory agreed with a grin. "And now you're quite possibly one of the most important people in the entire kingdom."

"The only thing is we can't just take it now. We're going to need an exit strategy, and we'll need cover, so he doesn't know what's happening. Because as soon as I break the spell, he's going to sense something is wrong."

"How much time would you need to take the real bow and swap in a fake before he realized something was off?" I pushed myself off the bed and rubbed at the nape of my neck.

"A couple minutes at least. What are you thinking?"

"What if there's some sort of distraction and everyone's focused on that while you're dismantling the spell?"

"That might work to make the switch, but he's still going to feel it."

"Oh, I think I get what you mean," Rory said. "You have to use blood to break the spell. So, we orchestrate something where you have to bleed in the vicinity of the bow. The spell comes down, we make the switch and then he'll think the weird feeling is just from the bloodshed."

"It's not the worst idea I've ever heard," she replied.

"How long would it take you to put the spell back on the fake?"

"It was intricate, and he cast it years ago. I'm not sure I remember all the steps."

"Then I guess you've got some homework of your own while we figure out how to manufacture a passable bow replica."

"The ceremony with Arthur is in less than twenty-four hours. I'm a quick study, but I'm not that good."

"We don't need it to be perfect. Just enough to fool him if he's not looking too closely."

"He knows what my magic feels like." The way darkness clouded her features and turned her tone sour told me there was a story to go along with it. One I hoped she'd share at another time.

"And you'll be building it back up. So, if he checks it, he'll sense your magic in place."

"Do you have any idea how to orchestrate this distraction?"

"How do you feel about playing a spurned lover to royalty?"

"And here I thought you were going to suggest something actually believable," she retorted.

"Oh, come on, you'd be a great catch."

"Which royal am I to have been spurned by then?"

"You did make a point of noting I came here with a prince."

"You have a lot of faith in his ability to act like he's in love with anyone, but you," Rory snickered.

Saoirse gaped at me. "You've caught the dragon's eye?"

"She's caught more than just his eye," Rory teased.

"Oi, shut it!" After an exasperated breath, I added, "There's something between us. It's new and undefined. Point is, he's been here before and it's possible you'd have interacted with him. It hasn't escaped either of you to notice that he is attractive. Other nobles are already falling over themselves to get his attention."

"I suppose I can play the role. But I'm not snogging anyone."

"Don't worry, you won't. Now, where exactly can we find a bow? We don't know how long it will take to make the forgery."

"The weapons that you'll need aren't going to be held in the armory. You're better off scouring the sheds on the edges of the archery pitch. It's where they leave old and broken equipment. You're going to want something that looks old enough to have been forged hundreds of years ago."

"Let me guess, that's where the games are currently unfolding?"

"I assume you can make yourselves hidden. No one will notice you slipping through the crowds. They'll all be focused on the nobility showing off for one another and trying to curry favor with the heir apparent."

"Assuming we get our hands on a bow, how are we supposed to get obsidian?"

"Leave that part to me. I've got a few ideas."

"Are you going to be missed in a few hours if we reconvene in our quarters?"

"No. I will be there. And I will not speak a word of this to anyone."

As she spoke, she held out a hand for me to shake. I met the gesture and squeezed her hand tight. "Thank you."

We stood with hands clasped together, neither wanting to be the first to relinquish their grip. Finally, I pulled my hand free and started for the door. Rory fell into step beside me, and I reached into my pocket for my phone. I pulled up the mapping app and found that our wandering and my impromptu detour into the dungeon had proved useful. It had mapped more of the castle than we'd intended. I could trace the route from where we were back to our quarters. Luckily, we were on the correct floor, just on the other side of the castle.

I walked confidently, as if I knew exactly where I was headed and with purpose until we reached our quarters. It was enough to fully orient me as to where we were meant to go. Rory still looked a little out of it as we descended the stairs to the first floor.

"I know this hasn't exactly gone like we'd planned."

"Considering we didn't really have a plan; I'd say it's not so bad."

"Yeah, that's not really what I'd intended."

"You're still learning to be a hero. It takes practice. And you are finding ways to bridge the gap between people who should be enemies."

"You don't think I'm being a fool for trusting her?'

Rory stopped walking halfway down the stairs. "Do I think that you're hoping her connection to the woman who raised you overrides a lot of bad blood? Yeah, that's pretty obvious. But I also think that we divide ourselves when we only focus on the differences between us. You're looking for what binds us together, our commonalities. That can't be a bad thing."

"To be honest, I can't entirely blame her for thinking I ruined her life in a way. Because ... some days that's how I feel about Arthur. And logically I know he didn't have a choice. He was a baby, too, when everything happened. And yet, the pure emotional side of me still thinks he's a fucking wanker for having what I was supposed to have."

"See, you're finding common ground."

It wasn't hard to find the archery pitch. All we had to do was follow the sounds of cheers and boos filtering through the openings of the courtyards. Before long, we were amongst a crowd of people watching as Arthur stood in the center of the pitch. He flashed a few women in the crowd a smarmy grin before letting loose not one but two arrows simultaneously. They struck separate targets on the far end of the field, just shy of center.

Show off.

I scanned the surroundings until I spotted a squat wooden structure nestled in some trees just behind the targets. My pulse quickened as I tried to find Uther. He was seated in a high chair on the far side of the pitch, his gaze laser-focused on Arthur's every move. Good. At least he was occupied for the moment. But that didn't mean the Seelie guards weren't on patrol.

"We need to find Taron," I whispered.

"Isn't it better to fill him in once we've got the bow?"

"Yes. But we're meant to be his entourage and security. No one should question if we're moving through the crowd to get near him. They'd just assume we're doing our job. Once we establish we're with him, we'll make our move."

By some small mercy, Taron, with Luanna still affixed to his arm like a permanent accessory, stood on the other side of the pitch, almost directly in front of the shed. Perfect.

FIFTEEN

Moving as quickly as I could, I led Rory around the edge of the crowd, making our way behind where Arthur stood, preparing to notch another pair of arrows into his bow. As we crossed behind him, I heard someone let out a wolf whistle that made him look up and flash another smarmy grin. He was loving being the center of attention. It didn't seem to matter whether he was the next in line to rule, he attracted fans. But for the moment, I was grateful that all eyes were on him. I sidestepped a beefy man wearing the Seelie court's colors, a sword dangling from a scabbard at his waist. For a split second I caught a glimpse of his face and could have sworn he was one of the soldiers sent to kill Nim and who'd tracked us through London on our quest to find the grail. But his cheeks were more sunken, and his eyes were the wrong color.

"Come on, we've got to keep moving," Rory urged.

Leaving the soldier behind, I wove my way past where Uther sat watching the festivities and took off at a steady pace until I reached Hagen. He looked thoroughly annoyed, and I immediately understood why. As I'd already seen, Luanna was wrapped around Taron's arm much like a barnacle. What I hadn't been able to gauge from my previous position was the fact she was talking almost nonstop; narrating the action on the pitch as if the people around her were blind.

"I'm not an archery expert, but I've never seen someone, even a royal, manage that move—" The twang of the bow being released cut her off as the arrows flew through the air, whistling as they neared their targets. As they'd done the last time, they split and hit the mark on two separate targets. "Let alone twice."

"He is probably using magic," I said in a low tone. It was enough to alert them to our presence without startling them.

"But that would be cheating," Luanna protested.

"Somehow I do not think the nobility, nor the

king would much mind a little cheating by the Crown Prince," Taron said. He locked gazes with me and concern washed over his face. He leaned in and whispered something in Luanna's ear. She relinquished her grip on his arm and Rory moved in to fill the gap he left in the crowd as he moved to stand beside me.

"You had me worried."

"Things got a little complicated. But the plan is moving forward."

"So, you obtained the materials needed?"

"Not quite." I hooked a thumb over my shoulder. "One piece is in there. But I'm going to need to get inside without anyone noticing."

He did a quarter turn and studied the structure behind us. "It appears the door is around the back. So, you should be able to slip in unnoticed."

"I'm sorry I disappeared for so long," I blurted as Taron urged me towards the shed.

"As you said, things have gotten complicated. I am sure you will tell me everything when the time is right. Now, go."

I waited until I was blocked by the row of targets before attempting any magic. I turned my focus inward and tugged it to the surface. Either there was still a bit of extra power from Excalibur in play or I was getting better at accessing my power through Talia's charms, because it rose without me having to exert much effort.

Hide me.

Almost like a cool wind, the air shifted around me, and I watched as my hands disappeared, followed by my arms up past my elbows. My clothes vanished next. The coolness settled around my head like a scarf, and I tiptoed to the back of the shed. My stomach did a flip as I pulled the door open. The hinges squeaked as the door shifted and a cloud of dust billowed from the confined space. No one had been inside for ages. Wonderful.

I barely managed to avoid a sneezing fit as I crossed the threshold and eased the door shut behind me. The space, despite the pale wood of the structure, was dark and musty. Tiny dapples of sunlight shone through gaps in the walls. Definitely not enough light to see by. Dropping the invisibility spell for the time being, I conjured a bit of greenish light, sending it up the ceiling to illuminate the cramped space.

Saoirse hadn't done the sheds justice. Piles of discarded weapons, some snapped in two, others missing strings and other bits and bobs were scattered across the space. Finding a usable bow in this mess could take hours if I was lucky.

"Avery, you still with me?"

"My butt hasn't left this chair in days."

"Do you have any images of the bow on your end?"

"I might, why?"

"Because I'm staring at a bunch of leftover weapons and if I choose something the wrong size, we're fucked."

"Oh, yeah let me see what I can find."

While I waited for her to locate the information I'd asked for, I started picking through the detritus. It turned out the Seelies had simply dumped anything that might have fallen into disrepair into the shed. I could almost hear Aunt Nim's voice in the back of my head, chiding me as a child for not keeping my room tidier. I'd always insisted it didn't matter since Jules was the one person who saw it and she didn't mind a little clutter. But the years of cleanliness she'd instilled within me flooded out and I found myself kneeling on the rough wood floorboards, organizing the arrows with a missing bit of fletching and the ones whose shafts had split in the middle.

"Looks like the bow is fifty-eight inches long," Avery said through the earring communicator.

"Sorry, going to need that in metric."

"Hang on...one hundred and forty-seven centimeters. Does that help?"

I closed my eyes, trying to picture the length in my head. It was nearly half a head shorter than me. "Yeah, I think so."

Casting about, I tried to find any bow that had remained intact. I skirted around some seriously dented shields to a pile of bows. A few had nasty char marks that I set aside. No need to try and cover up that kind of damage and make our lives that much harder. Rummaging through the pile, I finally hit upon one that looked usable. It appeared that the bowstring had come loose and sagged in the middle when I tried to draw it. That could be fixable, and I hoped Hagen or even Taron knew how to restring a bow.

I held it up to my side the long way and it seemed to reach the right place to be the proper length. I should have insisted we make a detour at the room for Talia's bag. As it was, I'd have to find a way to keep the bow hidden until we could return to the castle. Just as I slung the bow over my shoulder, a solid thump hit against the closed shed door. I froze in place, holding my breath. It could just be Taron coming to check on me or Rory. Maybe the archery was finished, and staff were coming to stow the used arrows?

I made a grasping gesture overhead and the globe of light made a lazy spiral towards my hands. I managed to grab hold and compressed it until it was just a tiny pin of light. I didn't need to blind myself when the door opened. Pressing my back to the nearest wall, I inched towards the entrance and held my right hand at shoulder height, balled into a tight fist. Slowly, I nudged the door open with my toe.

I lunged out of the shed and nearly tackled Hagen to the ground, my fist mere centimeters from his nose. He bucked me off in a fluid motion with his lower body and I tumbled into the grass. Scrambling to my feet I faced him. "You could have given me some warning it was you!"

"I thought it prudent to remain stealthy," he answered and kicked his legs up, letting the momentum carry him back onto his feet. He made the move look effortless and elegant. Damn dragons and their beauty, showing in everything they did.

As I shut the door to the shed, I realized that the ambient crowd chatter had died down. But I hadn't been in there long. Ten minutes maybe. I peered around the corner and found the archery pitch empty.

"Where's everyone gone?"

"Moved on to the next event. Hand to hand combat."

"What is it with everyone in this realm and fighting?"

"I suppose when you live extremely long lives, you get bored easily."

"Is Taron still with Lady Luanna?"

"Mercifully, no. She's left his company for now with the promise that they'll sit together at the banquet this evening. Oh ..." He studied my expression, and his lips twitched into a half smile. "And that absolutely infuriates you, doesn't it?"

"Only mad at myself for thinking it wouldn't annoy me."

"His highness has retired to his quarters. He asked that I ensure you meet him there for a debrief."

Somehow, I doubted either of them meant for it to be a little time with just the two of us. "Right then, let's go."

He gestured to the bow still slung over my arm. "I suggest you do something about that."

Concentrating, I waved a hand over the smooth

wood of the bow and around the loose string. Between one heartbeat and the next they shimmered out of sight. Now I needed to avoid running into anyone—a simple enough task. I surveyed our surroundings as he led me through a shrub-lined courtyard and into a different part of the castle I hadn't had a reason or a chance to map yet. I could pick out the sounds of more cheering as we passed through another open corridor and found ourselves back in the main receiving hall. From there, it was a quick trip up a floor and to Taron's room.

I didn't even have a chance to knock before it opened, and Taron appeared. He unceremoniously grabbed me by the forearm and yanked me inside the room. Slamming it shut behind me. I braced myself for what might come next. I did not expect to find Saoirse leaning against the window, back to the glass.

"Seriously, does this place have a different understanding of time? I wasn't gone that long this time," I said, laying the bow on the foot of the bed, and extricating it from the invisibility spell. I was getting pretty good at making my magic more of an extension of my being, letting it flow through and around me naturally—the way it was meant to be.

"I think it is time you explained what you meant

by complicated. Because I returned to find this woman waiting inside my room."

"You told me to act like we had something going on. And one of the guards spotted me while I was coming up here. I had to make it believable," Saoirse interjected.

"Where's Rory?"

"Doing a security sweep. She thought it would be better if the three of us handled this," Taron answered.

"Right, well, this is Saoirse. She's Nim's daughter. Short version, Uther fucked her life up as much as mine and she's meant to help us complete this insane quest. Oh, and her blood magic is the only thing that can get through the wards on the real bow. So, she's going to need to bleed and that's where all this comes in." I made a vague gesture between the two of them.

"Forgive me because I'm confused. You told me to woo the lady noble."

"I know. That's when I had thought any Seelie would do and she might have a little fun sticking it to the regent who ruined her party going plans. But she'll be suspicious if you all of a sudden give her the cold shoulder."

"So, your princess here thought it best to manufacture a lover's quarrel in open court," Saoirse noted.

"And when Uther realizes something is going on?" he prompted.

"We'll be standing by to make the switch and secret the real bow out of sight before anyone's the wiser. They'll never know its missing."

Taron opened his mouth to speak again, but Saoirse cut him off. "She wants me to recast the wards on the forgery."

"How'd you figure out how to do it?"

"I think I found references to the proper spells, but they take weeks to prepare. If I'm honest, I don't remember much about the king's work back then. I just went where I was told."

"Are there any spells you could throw up to make it look passable?"

"Maybe one or two."

"Well, that'll have to do."

I pointed to the bow I'd procured from the shed. "This is what we've got to work with."

Taron picked it up, turning it over in his hands. "I've seen worse."

I turned my attention to Saoirse again as he fiddled with the bowstring. "Any luck securing some obsidian?"

"Now that part was far easier to come by." She held up a tiny russet colored pouch and tossed it at me overhand.

I caught it and undid the drawstring, peering at the contents within. The chunks of shiny black gems glittered, enticing me to touch them. My gut said not to trust its beauty. I passed it back to Saoirse. "Here, you should probably hold onto this."

She pocketed the pouch without a word. "We need to practice this whole charade if we have any hope of making it a reality."

"I'm aware of that. You know the castle better than any of us. Where would you suggest we practice?"

"I think I have a place." She pointed to the weapon in Taron's hands. "I'll take that when you're done. It shouldn't take more than an hour to mold the obsidian."

Seriously. Waiting always felt like it took ages, and we didn't have that kind of time. But I wasn't about to complain to her face. Not when she was risking her entire existence to help us. Taron made a sound of satisfaction as he held the bow aloft. The string was perfectly taut. He raised the bow and pulled the string back as if about to fire and released it. It twanged in the air, but returned to its first position.

"You never cease to amaze me," I said, leaning over to plant a kiss on his cheek.

"I do aim to please."

Saoirse made a gagging noise as she took the bow from him and opened the door. "I hope you're ready for the hit to your reputation this is going to cause."

"Oh, I think I can withstand a bit of castle gossip."

SIXTEEN

The door shut, leaving Taron and I alone in his room. Unlike the night before, it didn't portend an intimate encounter. Even though he hadn't said it, I could feel his annoyance at being left in the dark. The way he held himself stiff shouldered told me I'd managed to upset him.

"Look, I know I should have run all this by you first," I said, turning to face him.

"I meant what I said. I can handle some idle gossip. It won't do any lasting damage to either me or my kingdom. It will soon be forgotten in the minds of the Seelie nobility. I'm not that interesting to them." His tone carried the notes of irritation his body language telegraphed.

"Maybe, but I just assumed you'd be willing to

go along with whatever I decided ... and that was wrong of me. Not being a very good leader if I can't even consider the feelings of my allies before I charge off headfirst into a plan."

"Not many leaders would openly admit when they're wrong." His tone was gentler this time.

"Yeah, well, I'm not feeling particularly like a leader right now. I jumped into this quest without a plan. I put people I care about in harm's way, even if indirectly. And I've risked multiple diplomatic incidents. Some princess I've turned out to be."

"You're feeling sorry for yourself," he assessed flatly.

"Damn right I am. I thought I was meant to do this. But I'm shit at it."

"All this proves is that you are above such deceptions. That is not a bad thing." He sat on the edge of the bed, leaning back on his hands. "It proves you are a decent person who is being forced to make uncomfortable choices for the greater good."

"I just want to finish this and get the fuck out of here. Their two-faced façade is rubbing off on me and it's making me cranky."

"No, that's your hunger," Gethin piped up in my ear.

"Don't suppose you could pop by with something to eat?"

"Come again?" Taron fixed me with a quizzical look until I pointed at my earrings. "Ah, our comrades back home offering their learned opinions. If they've assessed you operate less well when hungry, I concur."

"The banquet isn't that far off."

"You got kidnapped, assaulted, and climbed through who knows how much dust and grime. You deserve a proper meal now," Gethin chided.

"Fine, you have a point. Getting kidnapped and lightly tortured has sapped my strength a bit. I suppose I could do with some coffee and a sandwich."

"Hagen will accompany you," Taron said, clearly giving me no choice but to acquiesce. The fact he'd restrained himself and wasn't glued to my hip was a testament to his self-discipline.

"Because I need a chaperone?"

"You have been assailed once already today. It will not happen again I only wish it would not be unseemly for me to accompany you."

"I promise I'll have something to eat."

"Excellent." Taron's features softened even more

as he watched me. "How do you feel, having found Nim's daughter?"

"It's complicated. I'm happy she's alive. Grateful she's helping us and furious for what Uther put her through. I believe in my heart she's on our side. But I know it's not going to be as simple as sharing some compass-induced vision of her mum to fix it all. I promised her freedom when this was all over."

"So, you're hoping she'll come back to Camelot?"

"My gut says that's where she's meant to be. But I'm not going to force her. She's got to make that choice for herself. She's spent far too long doing the bidding of other people. That ends now."

"As much as I dislike the risk of your proposed plan to shed her blood, I do not see another option. But I'm afraid we may have to share more of our intentions with Lady Luanna."

"How much?"

"Having spent the better part of the day in her company, I can tell that she can talk anyone's ear off, but she is no actress. While not telling her the truth might make her reaction more genuine, she may cause more chaos or unpredictable behavior than we care for. I don't see another way but to convince her to help. And I'm honestly at a loss for how I'd explain dragging her into this practice run."

"Okay. We'll have to do the dry run during the banquet. Put in an appearance and the pair of you could slip away. Most people will have seen you together all day. They'll assume you've gone off for a bit of private time. We can fill her in then."

"You know, she is a rather interesting creature. Beneath the vapid exterior, she actually has some rather progressive ideas. I suppose that's why she was drawn to me. She doesn't want to follow in her parents' footsteps of marrying some lord she doesn't love simply to keep their bloodline fae."

"She's for equality. We should lean into that, then."

"You should go get that meal now," he urged, nudging me towards the door with his foot.

"And what are you going to be doing?"

"Putting on my best clothes to flirt with a pretty woman."

Leaving his room, I found Hagen waiting for me. Without preamble, he tugged my uniform into place, pivoted on his heel, and marched down the stairs. I hurried to keep pace with him.

"You're quiet." The silence between us was almost deafening by the time we had descended one floor to the kitchens.

"The prince may be willing to sully his reputation for your gamble, but I find it distasteful."

"It's his choice to make. If I had any other option, I'd take it. If you've got another answer, I'd love to hear it."

He shook his head, dark hair bouncing against the nape of his neck. "You should at least warn the royal family."

"Taron is a grown man. I'm fairly certain his parents can't dictate what he does, or who he does it with."

"My duty is to protect the family from any threat."

"I appreciate that. I like knowing he's safe and protected. But like I said, he knows what he's getting into. And he's also said that Seelie gossip doesn't last long. So, he's not worried about it. Therefore, I can't worry about it either."

"I can see why he's drawn to you. But I will admit my job was so much simpler before you came along."

I smirked. "Just think, if Uther hadn't gotten his way, you could have been dealing with this for decades."

"Humph."

I turned my attention to the kitchens. They

weren't dissimilar to the ones back in Camelot, save that everything was done in bright chrome to amplify the ambient light. It gave off the same aesthetic that everything was all shiny and pretty. Chefs gathered at one end of the space, arguing over what sounded like roast duck. A harried looking woman with a flour smear on her apron spotted me and approached, tucking dark blue strands of hair behind her pointed ears.

"Can I help you?"

"I'm afraid our duties kept us from eating earlier. We were hoping there might be some leftovers," Hagen answered.

"Coffee or a sandwich? Anything really," I added.

"Wait here. I'll see what we've got left. Can't promise much. We've already transitioned to preparing for the banquet."

"Really, anything's fine."

She gave a curt not and scurried across the room. I leaned on the nearest gleaming surface and caught the quasi-familiar reflection looking back at me. When the woman returned, she carried a cup, a small pot, and a tray of some leftover fruit tarts. "This is all I could scrounge up."

"It's perfect. Thank you."

I took a long sip from the coffee cup and let the

warm contents slide down my throat, igniting my synapses as the caffeine spread through my body almost instantly. Whatever faults the Seelie might have, they could make a damn good cup of coffee. Nibbling the closest tart on the tray, I watched the kitchen staff continue to hustle and bustle around the space, shoving enormous trays of biscuits into industrial ovens. They set pots of water to simmer on stovetops, with trays of vegetables chopped and prepped on sideboards. It all felt so normal. I could almost picture Gethin among their ranks, crafting delectable desserts and rich sauces to pair with the duck I'd heard mentioned earlier.

"You look a bit perkier," Hagen said softly.

"Food usually does that for me." I offered him one of the tarts, it looked to be made with raspberries and blackberries. He turned it down. "I have trained myself to conserve energy with the food I'm able to eat when off duty."

"Show off." I was tempted to wrap the tart and pocket it for later. I doubted the staff would notice or care.

I reached for a napkin sitting on the gleaming countertop to Hagen's left when I heard the door to the kitchen open. I stopped mid-motion as a slender woman with pale hair and bright blue eyes crossed the threshold. All motion in the room ceased the moment they realized she'd appeared.

"Highness," the woman who'd served me coffee said, dipping into a deep bow.

"No need to be so formal down here," she countered and slid onto a stool I hadn't noticed on the far side of the counter where I leaned.

"In front of guests, it is proper we address you accordingly," the woman said, casting Hagen and I a nervous look.

"Princess Aislinn," Hagen greeted, offering a brief bow.

Princess?

I studied the woman closer. She had a resemblance to Arthur in the cheek bones and facial structure, but she appeared more a carbon copy of the woman I'd seen at Uther's side the day before. So, Arthur had a sister. I wonder how she felt about her brother returning after all this time, to claim a throne she maybe thought was hers.

"You're new," she osaid, looking me dead in the face.

"She is still in training," Hagen said gruffly, with an accompanying light kick to my leg.

I dropped the napkin back on the counter,

offered a brief bow and stood straight. "Your Highness, it's nice to meet you."

She didn't offer her hand and neither did I. Apparently, royalty was above simple gestures like that. Instead, she turned back to the woman who'd been speaking. "Dolly, if there's any coffee left, I'd appreciate some."

"Right away."

"Forgive me for asking, but have all the festivities ended for the day?" Hagen was all politeness and proper etiquette.

"Oh, no they're still going. But I could only sit and watch men throw each other around like rag dolls for so long before I clawed my own eyes out."

"Surely the King and Queen would miss you?" I offered.

"If you're trying to be humorous, you need practice. I've become invisible since the golden child returned."

"Never thought I'd see the day a Seelie wasn't happy to have the prince back within their borders," I snorted.

"Not all of us are so willing to fawn over his every whim."

"He bump you out of your chance at the throne?"

"Mind yourself when addressing royalty!" Hagen

snapped. A wave of heat rippled from his skin as his anger bubbled to the surface.

Aislinn shook her head and a bit of the brightness in her gaze vanished.

"I was never going to take the throne. Father made certain of it. I'm not even positive he wanted me before I was born."

"Know your company, Princess," Dolly said with a disapproving glance in my direction.

"Why? The people have forgotten I exist," Aislinn continued as if the other woman hadn't spoken. "And so, I sit waiting for someone to notice me one day."

"I know it's not my place, but why not just leave?" I blurted.

She blinked at me, as if I'd just spoken in gibberish. "And do what exactly?"

I shrugged. "Whatever you wanted."

Dolly set a mug down in front of Aislinn and she picked it up without looking. She reached across the table and patted my forearm in a pitying gesture. "A princess doesn't just go where she pleases, no matter if she's noticed or not. One day, my father will have use of me."

"And you're okay with that ... being his pawn?"

She shrugged one slender shoulder and sipped

her coffee. "What are children but vehicles for their parents' aspirations?"

I bit my tongue to keep from saying something that might spark further argument. I filed the conversation away in the back of my mind. She clearly had no love for her brother and little affection for her father. I had no illusions about turning her against her own people. Though perhaps one day under the right circumstances she could prove to be an ally.

"There you are." Arthur's voice boomed from behind me.

I narrowly avoided smashing the coffee cup in my hand against the counter as I spun to look at him. My whole body went stiff under his scrutinizing gaze. I hadn't been this close to him since our bout where I'd forced him to reveal his true identity. I hated how he looked so comfortable in this place.

"I go where I please," Aislinn answered coolly.

"Father expects you at the banquet. You need to get ready. And you really should stop fraternizing with the staff. It's unbecoming for a person of your station."

Out of the corner of my eye I caught her raise her coffee cup. "When I'm done here, I'll get ready. Don't worry, *brother*, I won't ruin your special day. If you're lucky, he might actually give you a real gift when he names you heir in front of everyone."

Anger clouded Arthur's features, and I could read the tension in his neck as a vein pulsed. He was keeping himself in check because he didn't need the staff spreading tales that he'd lost his temper. He had an image to uphold. But as Aislinn finished her coffee, taking far more sips than necessary, I couldn't help but wonder what sort of gift she thought Uther might pass on to Arthur at the ceremony. What else could Arthur possibly need besides his father's blessing to cement his claim to the throne?

Hagen and I waited for the royal siblings to depart before making our way to find the rest of our party. We had a heist to practice.

SEVENTEEN

It wasn't hard to find our retinue. I just had to look for Luanna's vibrant locks. She was once again latched onto Taron's arm for dear life. Rory trailed behind them like some unwitting chaperone as the prince led the Seelie woman into the dining hall. Breath hitched in my throat when I walked in. The space had been expansive and luxurious this morning, but now it boasted floating candles suspended in mid-air overhead. Crystal chandeliers sparkled in the sunlight still streaming through the windows. It felt as though sunset was something arbitrary here. Hagen ushered me to a smaller table set off in one corner where other uniformed men and women sat squished together. Apparently, we were relegated to the children's table.

Uther stood at the head of the long table filling the room and raised his glass high. Those gathered around the table followed suit and waited for the king to speak.

"This has truly been a remarkable celebration. And I trust you will enjoy this evening's offerings. Eat, drink, enjoy. Tomorrow, we celebrate the true homecoming of my only son and bestow upon him his rightful honor as heir to the throne."

"Here, here!" a chorus of voices rang out around the room.

Uther snapped his fingers twice and the serving trays that had moments ago been empty filled with all of the vegetables and meats the kitchen staff had prepared. The scents mixed into a heady aroma that made my mouth water and my stomach gurgle with renewed hunger. The tarts had been a nice snack, but the small boost of energy they'd provided was used in the walk up from the kitchen. I turned back to our table to find it still barren.

"Oh, you've got to be joking," I muttered as a chair scraped against the stone floor and Rory sunk into the spot beside me.

"Apparently, we don't warrant a good meal until they've all had their fill," Rory said, matching my disappointment. "Back home, Gran always made sure we ate with our guests, family style."

"Cleary the Seelie don't have your gran's sense of generosity," I noted, chuckling to myself. The image of the older woman in the tartan shirt wielding a shotgun came unbidden to my mind's eye. She was not exactly what I would consider the generous sort, but her manners certainly trumped our current hosts.

"There will be time for food when we've completed our task," Hagen reminded us curtly.

"He's clearly never been hangry," I muttered.

As if my words had the power to summon, a single server appeared and made a beeline to our table. He carried a tray of thick rolls dotted throughout with what could have been sesame seeds. He barely had time to set the tray down before I scooped one up and bit in. It was dense and had a slight sourdough tang to it. The seeds turned out to be sunflower rather than sesame, which gave it an odd crunch.

"You are the most unladylike princess I have ever met," Hagen hissed in my ear.

I fixed him with a 'tough shit' look and turned my gaze to the high table. I watched as Taron leaned in and whispered something in Luanna's ear. The way her body tensed, I guessed he was asking her to sneak away with him. At least that part of the plan was in motion now. I had to remind myself it was just pretend. Even still, it was hard to see him flirt so easily with another woman. I scanned the room, hoping I'd spot Saoirse amongst the peripheral staff, but she was nowhere to be seen. That worried me. She'd insisted she had a location to practice our caper and yet hadn't given us the details.

Soon, the room filled with the sounds of cutlery hitting plates and voices falling into little pockets of conversation. It would be the perfect time to sneak away. Taron turned in his seat, met my gaze and offered a curt nod. His signal, it was time to get out of here. He held up his right hand and flashed me five fingers before turning back to Luanna. Interpreting it to mean I should give him five minutes before we followed, I turned back to the roll still sitting half eaten in front of me.

"What's going on over there?" Rory's question caught me off guard as I shoved a piece of roll in my mouth.

I followed her finger as she indicated the far end of the table where Aislinn sat beside Arthur, looking far more miserable than I'd seen her earlier. She'd done as he'd asked and changed her clothes, sporting a long flowing gown in an almost blood red color that dipped in a deep V in both the front and the back. The sleeves were off the shoulder and tapered to a point over her wrists. I even spotted a slender crown perched atop her pale hair, as if someone had woven it into the strands around it. Arthur looked as if he were gloating to her about something.

I didn't expect her to pick up her knife and thrust it into his face. The room fell silent at the display of imminent violence toward the prince. Uther, for his part, was on his feet in seconds with his right hand extended, fingers flared. Aislinn's body jerked, and her chair fell backward as it clattered nosily to the floor. She clawed at her throat, the knife falling from her grasp as she did so. The king's usual superior expression had morphed into one of pure rage.

"How dare you assault the heir to the throne." His voice was a rasp and yet the room amplified his words for all to hear.

I turned my attention to the queen, who still sat silently beside her husband. I could read the pain in her expression, barely keeping her emotions in check as he railed against the young woman who looked so much like her mother. Slowly, Aislinn's face turned red and then took an unnatural purplish-blue tinge. He was choking her out.

"Why isn't anyone doing anything?" I whispered to my companions.

"Because it isn't our place to tell a king how to punish his subjects, especially his own children," Hagen answered.

Finally, Arthur stood and held out a hand towards his father. "It was a little prank. Father, there is no need to spoil our evening because she could not accept a joke. Just send her away, but let's enjoy the rest of the evening with all of our guests."

Uther's eyes bulged in his head at Arthur's request, but after a breath, he lowered his hand and Aislinn's body dropped to the floor. She grabbed for the edge of the table in an effort to steady herself. Two servants appeared almost out of thin air and escorted her from the room. I could have sworn one of them was Dolly, the cook from earlier.

Uther took a moment to regain his composure before he reclaimed his seat and dug into his roast duck as if nothing had happened. The conversations that rose up around the table carried a more hushed quality this time. No one wanted to be caught discussing the king's outright assault on his own child. And yet, it was the most exciting thing to happen all day.

Amongst the chattering, I watched Taron excuse himself and step away from the table. A moment later, Luanna followed suit. Our clock started now. I was more than ready to be as far from the king and his temper as I could get.

Finally, after what felt like ages, Hagen nudged my foot and I slipped away, with Rory hot on my heels. I prayed anyone who saw us leave would simply assume we'd gone off to find our prince. Technically, they weren't wrong. We made it to the main entry hall before I felt a hand clamp down on my left arm. I spun to find Saoirse, her face obscured by an elaborate cloak.

"Hurry up." She took off speed walking, the cloak flowing out behind her in dramatic fashion.

Rory and I exchanged a look, but hurried to catch up with her. When she stopped, we found ourselves standing outside the room with all the creepy Seelie portraits.

"I'm not sure this is going to work." I gestured to the portraits. "They're following me everywhere I walk. It's creepy."

Saoirse let out an annoyed huff. "No one comes

in here for that very reason. Not even the king. It's about the right size to mimic the throne room."

"What about ... you know, the thrones and stuff?" Rory pointed to the barren nature of the room.

"I've got that covered." Saoirse held up both hands, palms out and closed her eyes. The cloak's hem rippled as if caught in a stiff breeze and the air around us grew thick. I could almost pick out a floral scent in the air as the walls took on the same rippling effect. The portraits vanished one by one, replaced with the ornate adornments of the throne room. Where the space had been empty, large thrones towered over us. A thick red carpet rolled out down the center of the room and on the far wall sat the bow, secured by its iron brackets to the wall.

"You're good." I couldn't hide the awe in my tone. There was no way I could have pulled off something this intricate. Not without a lot of time and preparation.

"I know."

"You're sure we can go in here?" Luanna's voice filtered down the corridor.

"Yes, we won't be missed," Taron answered. "And no one is going to come looking here. You have my word."

They rounded the corner and her eyes went wide, first in surprise and then confusion. "But ... the throne room's that way." She pointed behind her.

"You were supposed to explain things," I addressed Taron sharply.

"I was getting there—" he began, but Luanna cut him off with a squeak of shock.

I spun, hands balling into fists on instinct to find Aislinn standing there. "Since when do rooms in this place move?"

I expected Saoirse to make up some excuse, but she stood there in stunned silence at the princess's sudden appearance.

"Do something," Rory rasped.

"Prince Taron was hoping to offer Arthur a special gift at the ceremony tomorrow and Saoirse was kind enough to help us set up a space to ensure it could be done safely," I blurted.

Taron mouthed the words 'what gift?' and I gave him a 'just go with it' hand gesture.

"Not what I would have expected. Your kind aren't exactly our biggest fans," Aislinn noted.

"We are pragmatic. We can see the value of being in the good graces of the next monarch of your realm."

"You don't seem to care for him much," she said, and I stepped a little closer.

"He casts a long shadow." She gave Taron a once over. "You know, you wouldn't be faulted if whatever gift you present has a bit of bite." After a moment, she added, "Or burn."

"I assure you Princess, I have no desire to spark war with your family."

"Pity. It might make things a little more palatable around here." She waved her hand dismissively. "Just make sure you put it back how you found it."

Taron offered her a deep bow from the waist and watched her walk away. When he turned to face me, I could see actual worry in his eyes. "What was *that*?"

"I panicked."

"You weren't planning to give the prince a gift then?" Luanna looked baffled.

"We don't need her for this," Saoirse declared, approaching Luanna with her hands raised.

I moved to intercept her. "Hang on. What do you think you're doing?"

"Removing a variable from the equation. We can complete this without her. She would only make matters ... messier."

"Maybe she's right.," Rory piped up.

I glared at her. "How so?"

"The circle of people who knows what's going on is already bigger than we'd intended. Having her involved means we risk something going wrong."

"What are you all on about?" Luanna demanded.

"We're planning to steal that fancy bow from the throne room, and we need you to pretend to be horribly offended when Taron here has a tense interaction with a spurned lover of old," I said in one breath.

Luanna faced Taron. "You've been using me?"

"I am afraid so."

The look of confusion and hurt shifted to a look of pride. "How very Seelie of you."

"I fear that is not the compliment you hope it to be."

"I came here all annoyed I was missing the fun I had planned. My brother never would have gotten involved in a plot to trick the king."

"You realize if you help us, you risk being imprisoned, or worse?" Saoirse's tone was dead serious.

"But if we succeed, oh we'd be legends. Maybe then my parents would let me do what I wanted."

"Now that we're all on the same page, we need to get this going. I doubt we're going to get this right on the first try."

Saoirse closed the door to the room and traced an intricate knot design onto the doorknob. It glowed a vivid green before fading, leaving the outline of the knot behind. "We'll have until sunrise."

"Let's hope we don't need that long."

Saoirse produced the bow from a fold in her cloak and I could see obsidian encrusted on the shaft in the ambient light. If I were looking at it from a distance, I wouldn't have been able to tell it apart from the original.

"I think you've missed your calling," I said with a grin. "That is bloody brilliant."

She pointed to the thrones at the far side of the room. "They should have bystanders within about three feet of the throne. Uther doesn't like anyone getting that close to him. I suppose it makes sense he'd be paranoid about someone trying to stab him in the back."

"That's going to be a problem. We need to get right up to it," Rory pointed out.

"That's why we need to make it look believable," I reminded her and pointed at Luanna followed by Saoirse. "You're going to need to make her bleed."

Luanna flashed a toothy grin. "Oh, I can do that."

"Here goes nothing."

We lined up along the wall closest to the bow and I watched as Saoirse approached Taron. I tried to tune out the fake argument that ensued. Luanna for her part stepped in quickly and gave Saoirse a solid shove in the chest, enough to send her staggering back. Though not hard enough to draw blood.

"Come on, you can do better than that," she taunted.

Luanna reached out and struck Saoirse across the face. A thin vein of blood welled up and dripped down her cheek. "Better."

She waved her hand over her face and the wound vanished. "We're only going to have a small window to do this." She addressed me. "The moment this starts, you need to be unseen. The king will only tolerate disruptions for so long."

She didn't need to remind me. I had seen and knew what his temper could do.

EIGHTEEN

Eight ... nine ... ten. I counted off in my head until the squabbling began again. We'd finally managed to choreograph it, so Rory moved to block me from of the thrones as I wrapped myself in invisibility. I moved with quick steps to position myself at the bow, ready to make the switch as soon as Saoirse stumbled my direction, blood dripping from her mouth. She wiped it from her lips and held her hand out long enough for me to feel her magic connect with mine. Together, we directed it onto the wards keeping the bow secured to the wall. The iron brackets loosened enough at the top for me to slip the bow free and replace it with our replica.

Now came the complicated part. In the span of about forty seconds, Saoirse needed to cast enough of a spell on the fake to fool Uther while also keeping his attention focused elsewhere.

"Your spell is slipping," Luanna said breezily.

I blinked, unsure who she was addressing until I spotted my right foot sticking out of nothingness. No, I'd gotten distracted watching Saoirse weave the spell.

"Damn it."

"We've been at this for hours," Rory complained, pointing to the fact that her phone read 4 in the morning. My eyes started to go bleary the longer we pushed through.

"We aren't going to have another chance to practice this," Saoirse insisted. "We go again."

"We are not going to be able to make this believable if we are not rested," Taron declared, his tone all authority.

Saoirse let out a long sigh. "Fine. But we still haven't managed to do it successfully once yet."

"We got pretty close the last time." I tried to muster some positive energy. "And we know where we tend to struggle."

"Your focus," Luanna answered cattily.

"Which won't be an issue if I can actually get a decent night's sleep."

Taron gave me a wounded look as Saoirse

released the magic around us. It popped like a soap bubble and the change in the air made me momentarily woozy. I managed to stay upright as the throne room walls faded back into their creepy portraits. I stifled a yawn as I handed the fake bow back to Saoirse. She shook her head and pushed it back at me.

"Better it remain with you."

In case I got caught, she could disavow any knowledge of the whole thing. It made a modicum of sense. Stowing the bow in Talia's bag, I secured it to my belt and raked my fingers through my hair.

"Right, the ceremony is at noon so we should make sure we're all in place by half past eleven."

Luanna gave a giddy giggle as she left the space. Rory followed after her, leaving Taron, Saoirse, and I in the room. She looked at me. "You meant what you said to me. About going where I choose ... after."

"Yes. Though I'd be lying if I said I wasn't hoping you'd come back to Camelot with us. I know we're not family by blood, but I feel like we've missed a lot of time together and it's easier to make up for it if we're together."

"I'll consider it."

"That's all I ask."

She hurried from the room. And then there were

only two of us. Taron wrapped his arms around my waist and leaned in to plant a kiss on my lips. I pressed my palms against his chest to halt the motion. "As much as the idea is enticing, I am really dead on my feet. And Luanna wasn't wrong. I was the one who kept slipping up."

"You are trying to cast delicate magic while concealed with another powerful being's enchantments. It's bound to be harder than what they're doing."

Part of me wished I could just take off the pendant and remove the barrier of dragon magic. But as far as anyone in the Seelie court knew, I was back home in Camelot. Only Saoirse knew the truth and that was a risk in and of itself. Part of me argued that I'd be under the invisibility spell. No one would be the wiser. But it was entirely possible Arthur or even Uther might recognize my magic if it weren't hidden by Talia's. Stupid logic winning out.

"I'll be fine. I just need some sleep. I promise once we're out of here, we will have plenty of time for where you were heading." I kissed him on the lips for good measure.

"At least let me escort you back upstairs."

"That would be nice."

Thankfully, even the castle staff were sound

asleep as we ascended the staircase. He dropped me off at the room I shared with Rory. He offered me a deep bow and I gave him a curtsy before parting ways. Rory was already asleep, snoring soundly as I eased the door shut behind me and stripped out of the uniform. The bed felt like heaven as I sunk into the mattress and my head hit my pillow.

Water burbled somewhere off to my right and I found myself in the peaceful stretch of forest by the river. Aunt Nim stood alone this time. I approached and the grass muffled my footfalls. When she turned, anxiety pinched the skin around her eyes and for the first time in a long time, her ears were tapered to points.

"You know, I'm grateful for these afterlife visits, but I'm not sure how restful this one is going to be," I noted.

"I am concerned that what you are endeavoring to do will fail."

"So, we haven't nailed it perfectly yet. We'll get it."

"The risks you are taking are great."

"Don't blame me. I didn't choose this. The universe beckoned and I've learned when that happens, I follow."

"There is something you are missing, dear child. Something I cannot see. But I feel it."

"What sort of feeling?"

"Danger. Betrayal."

My stomach did a flip. Maybe Saoirse had been right

in the first place. Maybe bringing Luanna in on the scheme was a mistake. But what if Saoirse turned out to be the one who betrayed us to a king who'd dictated her movements her entire life. I had no way of knowing whether she'd told him the truth in between our meetings.

"Whatever it is, I'm going to get through it. I know you're trying to help, but you've got to trust that I can handle whatever is coming. I'm the chosen one after all, remember."

"Not all those chosen for power live to wield it."

"Thanks for the pep talk Aunt Nim. Really, aces."

"You long ago grew out of being coddled, Morgan. Be vigilant."

I woke with a sense of dread twisting my stomach into a knot. Despite my phone saying I'd slept for five hours straight; I didn't feel rested. Aunt Nim's little dream visit had been more distressing than I think even she had intended. A soft knock on the door drew me out of bed. Rory was nowhere to be seen. I eased the door open a few inches to find Taron on the other side.

"You look awful."

"Just what every woman wants to hear from the man they're sleeping with," I muttered.

"Did you rest at all?"

"I was unconscious for a bit. Had a doomsday visit from Nim though." I opened the door wider to let him enter. "She thinks someone is going to betray us."

"Not to speak ill of the dead, but it seems rather unnecessary to put such thoughts in your head."

"Believe me, I could have gone without it, too. But now I keep thinking what if she's right? I mean, we just met Luanna and Saoirse in the last forty-eight hours. We don't really know that much about either of them. And as Luanna revealed, the Seelie like a bit of manipulation, even when it's happening to them."

"That is certainly a possibility. As is Saoirse changing her mind or sabotaging your efforts in some other manner. But she seemed genuine about wanting a fresh start away from this place."

"I know. And that's where I get hung up. I want to believe that they're both genuine and that I can trust them. God, I want to believe that to my core, but with Uther and Arthur around, it feels like I'm waiting for the other shoe to drop. Almost like we've been lucky so far, but it can't possibly last."

"Just a few more hours and we will take our leave, with the bow in our possession."

"Oh, you might want to come up with something to present to Arthur. I have a feeling Princess Aislinn may be keeping an eye on our little fib."

"It is lucky that I have the ability to fly." He reached into his pocket and produced a deep purple gem set into a thick brown leather strap. I could see a place to attach the scabbard for a sword.

"It's pretty."

"Fairly common among our nobility. But seeing as he's never been to any of our formal dignitary functions, if I tell him, it is a priceless family heirloom, he'll be none the wiser."

"It should frighten me how good you are at this. But it just makes me want to kiss you," I professed.

"You'll hear no argument from me."

I pulled him close and felt his arms wrap tight around my waist. He rested his forehead against mine and I stared into his eyes. I could get lost in their depths for ages. It seemed a nice, safe alternative to the madness we were about to attempt. One of these days I was going to have a nice long stretch where my life and the lives of my friends weren't in peril. Too bad today wasn't that time.

Taron kissed me softly on the lips and I felt the heat from his body wash over me. A promise of what awaited us once this was over. I was going to hold him to it.

Reluctantly, I pulled away. "See you down there. I need a shower and a change."

"Be mindful of the time."

"Yes, Mum," I teased and swatted him on the arm as he left the room.

The door closed with a soft click, and I rummaged in Talia's bag for clean clothes. I hadn't realized Talia had packed me a slightly less formal uniform. A little note pinned to the tunic let me know it was meant for today's event. Helpful. Making certain I had her bag with the faux bow with me, I retreated to the shower and let the water wash away the unease the dream with Aunt Nim had stirred up.

As I dressed, I longed for Jules to give me a pep talk. She'd always had my back, and I felt out of sync without my best friend. I never thought I'd be going off on all these adventures without her by my side. And not knowing if she was any better was going to distract me. Lucky for me, I had a convenient way to check up on her. Pulling my hair into a knot at the nape of my neck I said, "Avery, you there?"

"She finally laid down for a nap and something to eat," Gethin answered in my ear.

"And what about you?"

"Don't worry, Emerys has made sure I take care of myself."

"And Jules? Any change?"

"The doctors say she's stabilized now. They couldn't quite figure out what was causing the wounds to keep reopening, but it's stopped now."

"That's a relief."

"But she's not woken up yet."

That wasn't the news I'd hoped to hear. "Well maybe now her body's done fighting off whatever was making her ill. It just needs time to rest and recover." I was trying to convince myself as much as him that my words were true.

"I know I shouldn't have been listening, but I heard what you said about your aunt warning you of danger."

"I want to ignore it, but I know it would be foolish not to heed her advice."

"Well, I mean, technically speaking she wasn't giving you advice. More likely it was your subconscious mind working through your own emotions."

"This isn't the first time I'd had a visit like that from Aunt Nim since she died."

"Just try to get out of there in one piece, please."

"Promise I'll do my very best." My phone's clock ticked over to quarter of eleven. My chat with Taron and the shower had eaten up more time than I'd realized. "I've got to go. But if everything goes to plan, I'll see you in a few hours."

Making sure the bag was looped securely through my belt and hidden from view by the hem of my tunic, I made my way to the first floor. I found Hagen waiting for me. He didn't speak as he led me toward the throne room. A large collection of the nobility already stood outside the room waiting to gain entry.

"We're early," I whispered as Hagen pushed the door inward.

"Prince Taron's presence has been requested by the king."

My mouth went dry, and my feet stopped responding to my brain's signals to move forward. Hagen gave me a solid shove between the shoulder blades, and I staggered forward. Sweat prickled along my hairline as I scanned the space in front of me. Taron stood to one side, hands grasped behind his back, and head held high. He faced the thrones at the far end of the room where Arthur lounged, one leg thrown over the arm like he were sitting watching television at home. The smug expression on his face roused my desire to punch him in the face. Uther was nowhere to be seen.

Trying to remember I was meant to be part of the dragon security force accompanying Taron, I hurried to stand just off to his side and a step behind. Taron remained still and silent as Arthur surveyed him.

"I know the servants told you my father wished to see you, but that was a lie," Arthur explained, boredom dripping from his words.

"As I can see," Taron said, his posture remaining stiff as a statue. "Your honors are not for another hour. So, please tell me why you've dragged me in here."

"A little birdie told me you had something to give me."

Seriously?

Aislinn had told Arthur about the made-up gift from Taron, and he insisted Taron give it to him in private? What purpose did that serve? From behind the thrones, I heard a door open, and I craned my neck to see who'd entered the room. Someone let out a growl as two pairs of footsteps sounded on the stone flooring. Saoirse appeared sporting a black eye and busted fat lip. Aislinn rounded the far edge of the unoccupied throne beside Arthur.

"I told you we had a spy in our midst," Aislinn said, pointing at Saoirse. "She's conspiring with him to rob you of your moment. Of the gift Father intends to give you."

Saoirse straightened and wiped the blood from her lip. "I am so sorry. She gave me no choice." She swallowed before adding, "Uther intends to gift Arthur with the Obsidian Bow to cement his claim to the throne."

What? I couldn't have heard her correctly. Uther intended to gift Arthur the bow ... to use. Had that been his intention all long or had some part of our plan made it to the king's ears after all? And how the hell did Aislinn know what was going on? To his credit, Taron looked unfazed by the sudden change of circumstances.

"You are clearly mistaken, Princess," Taron said and finally unclasped his hands to gesture to Rory, who held out the jeweled belt. "I did come intending to offer your brother a gift. Worn by many of my people's greatest rulers. It brought them luck in battle. It felt like an appropriate gift to honor you taking your rightful place."

Arthur stared down his nose at the proffered gift. "You think I am a fool. I know you have been colluding with Camelot's little bitch, the lost princess. Tracy, is it? Or Emma? It's hard to keep track of all the lies."

"Unless I am mistaken, her highness is not in this room. And I am being pragmatic. I can see that tensions are high. I intend to keep my people on the winning side."

"You aren't as good a liar as you think," Arthur said and slid off the throne, standing to his full height. He was still a hair shorter than Taron, even as he moved to stand toe to toe with the dragon prince. "You were after the bow. I can only imagine what you thought you might do with it."

"Defend myself from enemies, I'd expect. That's usually what weapons of war are for."

"I thought you were all about history," Aislinn noted, head cocked to the side as she studied Taron. "Isn't that what you told that vapid noble woman while you wined and dined her?"

"You are implying I don't know your relic's origins. I confess, I do not know your kingdom's conquests as well as my own."

"The Obsidian Bow can find its mark no matter

the distance. And it can only be wielded by a Seelie," Arthur chimed in.

"Maybe he just wanted a pretty trophy on his wall, like your father," Saoirse spat.

"How dare you speak to me in that tone," Arthur bellowed and moved to strike her.

I acted on instinct, throwing myself in the line of his assault. I caught his hand between both of mine and it was enough to send him off balance. I ached to draw Excalibur and give the prick a rematch of the last time we'd faced off. But revealing myself wasn't the best move in this moment. Our plan was no longer viable, but a new plan was beginning to solidify in my mind. I had to trust that the people in the room I'd come to call allies would follow my lead.

"You really have daddy issues, don't you? I mean he literally sent you away to be raised by someone else all because he thought it would benefit him politically," I taunted. "I mean, sure you'd have the title of king, but you'd still have been his puppet."

"Silence!" Arthur howled, hand slicing through the air. Electricity crackled from his fingers, and I narrowly dodged the attack.

The energy hurtled through the space, striking

the far wall with a sizzle. In the process of avoiding the electricity, I'd knocked Saoirse to the floor. I knelt beside her and said, "Do you trust me?"

"More than that lunatic at the moment."

"You need to bleed on that weapon. I'll keep him distracted. Go."

"Aislinn is still a fighter, too."

"Good thing I'm not alone then. And once you've freed it, I need you to set it on the floor."

"What?"

"Just go with it. I promise everything will make sense."

I turned back to face Arthur to find Taron and Hagen engaged in a face-off with Aislinn. She'd produced braided whips made of pure energy and writhing thorny vines that lashed out at them. Hagen threw himself in front of Taron to deflect the blow, the skin on his right forearm shifted into rough scales.

"You remind me of her," Arthur said, taking a swing at my head.

This time I wasn't fast enough to dodge the blow and stars exploded in my vision. "Not sure who you mean," I coughed.

"Camelot's precious lost heir."

"You realize she was innocent in all of this. Your mad father decided infanticide was a good idea."

"He is my king."

"Blind loyalty like that will get you killed." The vibrant red color of the carpet gave me another idea and I pictured the fabric igniting, rising up in a thick wall of flame. It obscured everything around it as I advanced on Arthur. The flames danced higher until they reached the ceiling, and smoke began to coil out around us. Arthur's eyes were wild as he struggled to get his bearings.

I didn't bother trying to orient myself. He'd always have the upper hand in that department. But I took a deep breath and listened. Lime zipped along my tastebuds as my magic enhanced my hearing. I could pick out individual bits of fabric rustling with movement as Taron continued to occupy Aislinn's attention. But more importantly, I listened for the sound of metal prying loose from stone. The subtle whine and the pop of power released when Saoirse undid the bindings on the bow.

For a long moment all I could hear was the crackle of the flames around me.

Come on, come on.

Finally, the sound of metal clattered down low,

and a bright purple light split through the flames, shining as I caught a glimpse of Saoirse holding the bow aloft. Light sparkled in her eyes, and I could almost feel the magic radiating from within her. The weapon called to me, promising me power through her.

I shook my head to clear my thoughts. No, she was not something to be used. Not anymore. The flames parted and I saw her set the bow down just as I'd asked.

Don't burn me.

With the magic fueling the fire still at my command, I raced through and bent down, tugging Talia's bag open. I felt the tip of the fake bow within reach and pulled it free. The obsidian glittered in the firelight and as I laid it down on the ground beside the real version, I almost couldn't tell the difference. I trusted it would fool Arthur and Aislinn, at least long enough for us to get out of here and back to safer ground.

I locked eyes with Saoirse and did my best to share my thoughts with her. *'We need to mark the real one, so we know we've got what we came for.'*

'Take it. It will obey you.'

I shook my head. *'It's meant to be wielded by you, not me.'*

Without warning, Saoirse grabbed my hand and drew a blade across my palm. It stung the moment she squeezed the wound and forced my blood to drip onto the real bow. Blood rushed to my head as if I'd stood too quickly and I watched the red droplets take on a decidedly green tinge before they shimmered and disappeared into the obsidian surface.

'Call to your magic and it will respond now.'

I kicked the fake bow through the fire in Arthur's general direction. I knew I should simply secret the real bow away, but I needed to keep him distracted a little while longer. I didn't have an exit strategy yet. Just as I stood, a violent wind swept across the room, and I toppled backwards. The fire I'd started vanished and Uther stood there, looking indignant that I'd dared to sully his precious throne room. Arthur stopped his assault the moment his father entered the room. Aislinn, however, seemed unaware of his presence as she flung herself at Rory and Hagen, trying to take them both to the floor by sheer force of will.

Much like he'd done the night before, Uther thrust out a hand and Aislinn went flying backwards, her body contorting like a bizarre rag doll until she stood straight. "How dare you enter my home and assault my children."

"They started it," I said before I could stop myself.

Uther acted as if I hadn't spoken. To him, I was a lowly servant, not worth his attention. He rounded on Taron. "I suppose your kingdom is lucky it did not send its next monarch. I do wonder how long they'll mourn you." He turned to Arthur. "I suppose now is as good a time as any to try your new gift. I would say don't miss, but it isn't possible."

He retreated back through the door I now realized still sat open behind the thrones, dragging Aislinn with him. Fury burned in her gaze as she moved in stiff, robotic motions behind her father. Although I didn't have time to worry about her fate. If Arthur got his hands on the real bow, we were fucked. Thankfully, Arthur made a lunge for the fake.

Not wanting to make it too easy for him, I summoned a globe of greenish light and lobbed it at him. It smashed into the floor like an oversized raindrop, but it temporarily blinded him, even as he scrambled for the bow. How he intended to use it without arrows was a mystery I hoped I didn't have to solve. Taron, Rory, and the others closed ranks around me. It took everything I had not to push Taron aside to keep him beyond range.

"Any idea how we get away from here?" Rory asked.

"Flying is out," Hagen answered. "Shifting takes time and they could gain reinforcements by then."

"Then we make a run for it," I said. "Get as far as we can from the castle, and I'll see what I can do from there."

"Take the corridor in front of the throne room all the way to the left. There will be a door that leads to the stables. The castle wards are weakest there," Saoirse said just as Arthur scooped up the fake bow.

With a flourish, a series of arrows materialized in a quiver on Arthur's back. He nocked the first one and trained it on Taron's chest. "I'm going to enjoy this."

A fresh wave of panic set in as I pictured the arrow finding it's mark and ending things between us. I refused to let that happen. He needed a new target. Something he wasn't expecting. Out of the corner of my eye, I watched Saoirse bend down and retrieve the real bow, secreting it behind her back.

Well, here went everything.

I yanked the pendant from around my neck, feeling the clasp break as it came up against the base of my skull. The moment the necklace was no longer touching my skin, the spell shimmered out of existence. Gasps went up from my companions in the room as my pallor lightened and my facial features shifted slightly.

"So, about that whole me not being in the room bit. Yeah, that was a lie." I stepped in front of Taron. "Come on then, pretty boy. Let's see what that thing can really do."

Arthur stood there, staring at me as if he weren't sure he was seeing me. I stepped even closer as I heard both Hagen and Rory groan and slammed my fist into Arthur's face. "That is for being a pompous arsehole and a twat to your sister."

Blood trickled down his face as he backpedaled and raised the arrow at my face. Now seemed the right time to bring out my own magical weapon and in a blink, Excalibur materialized in my right hand, ready to deflect his attacks.

Anger clouded Arthur's features, and he let the arrow fly in my direction. My blade deflected it instantly. He fired another with the same result. Confusion quickly overtook him as he stared at the bow. He was clearly wondering how I could parry his shots when the bow was meant to find it's mark magically, no matter what.

"I think the stories might have exaggerated things," I taunted, slowly positioning myself to have a clear sprint to the door.

"I don't need a magic bow to end you," he spat and aimed the bow off to my right.

I stared as he let the arrow loose. I expected it to slam into the wall. Instead, the arrow ricocheted off the stonework and slammed into the floor mere inches from Taron's feet. Right, he may have cheated at the archery competition, but he had to have some skill to make it look good. Time to get the hell out of this place.

I raised my free hand and conjured a thick wall of mist, hoping my companions understood it was time to run. Thankfully, by the tread of running feet moving past me, they'd picked up on my signal. We burst through the doors to find the assembled nobles standing around in disarray gawking at what was happening. I saw guards trying to force their way through the throng in order to reach us, but the nobles seemed unwilling to move. I used the crowd to my advantage and ducked between bodies, pushing through in the direction Saoirse had suggested. Even as we cleared the crowd, arrows flew overhead, trying to land on their marks. I barreled through the first door I saw and found myself standing amongst sleek white horses with deep brown eyes. The stables just as Saoirse had promised.

Pulse quickening as more arrows rained down on us, I sketched a circle in the air. I pictured the first place in this realm I'd ever felt safe and dove through, praying my companions followed suit.

CHAPTER

TWENTY

My heart hammered in my chest as the portal closed behind me. I threw myself to the ground, arms flung over my head as I waited for hell to rain down. But nothing came. I blinked and slowly took in my surroundings. The tall trees of the wooded area near the Crystal Cave rose up over-head. The brush and brambles scraped at my arms as I tried to sit up and take a breath to steady my pulse. We were back in Camelot.

"Everyone okay?" I asked, my throat suddenly raw, as if I'd been screaming for a prolonged period.

"I believe we have an unintended guest," Hagen said, hauling Saoirse to her feet and shoving her against a nearby tree.

I scrambled to my feet and swatted his hands away. "Stop. She's with me."

Hagen's eyes bulged as he studied the Seelie woman, his jaw working as if he were trying to choose his words carefully. Smart man. Finally, he said, "You invite danger into your court, Princess."

"She's family," I proclaimed before Saoirse could speak. "And I won't hear another word about it. Now, we need to get out of here before they realize where we went and come looking."

"Uh, not sure that's going to be a good idea." Rory's voice came out in a croak, and I pivoted to see her. She stood with her whole body swaying as her hand gripped the shaft of an arrow Arthur had loosed from the forged bow. The arrowhead was lodged between her ribs. The fact she was still conscious and upright was a bloody miracle.

"Oh, shit."

"I can get her back to your castle," Taron offered, already reaching for the hem of his shirt.

Much as I might have enjoyed the show, flying with Rory in such a state wasn't safe. Taking a steadying breath, I traced the circumference of a circle midair, picturing the infirmary where I'd last seen Jules. The castle interior popped into existence within the confines of my spell. "This is faster."

Hagen released his grip on Saoirse, and she moved to support Rory's weight, the real obsidian bow slung across her torso. Our gazes met and I could swear they reflected affection. It disappeared a split second later as she stepped through the portal. I could already hear the clamoring of medical staff attending to the sudden arrival of the wounded. No doubt there would be guards descending the moment anyone realized Saoirse's heritage.

I pulled Taron close. "Thank you for risking everything for me on this one."

"It seems to continue to escape you that where you go, I will follow," he said and kissed me hard on the mouth.

I held onto that feeling and the weight of his body pressing against mine for as long as I could, before relinquishing him. I turned to Hagen. "Thank you for having my back. Get him home safe."

"I would not fail in my duty to protect him this close to the end of such an exhilarating quest."

"Morgan?" Avery's voice rang out through the portal. The hint of panic in her tone was enough to pull me away completely from the dragons in the forest.

I stepped through the portal, bracing myself for

the chaos that awaited me. The spell blipped out of existence the moment my feet touched the floor, and I took in the scene before me. Rory now lay on a bed, propped up by pillows as a doctor and nurse prodded the arrow's entry. Avery's cheeks were pale as she glanced between me and Rory.

"We lost contact," she said, pulling her glasses off and pinching the bridge of her nose.

"Sorry. Things kind of went pear-shaped there at the end and we had to make a run for it." I spun in an arc, looking for our newest addition. Saoirse stood off to one side, bow now clasped firmly in both hands. "But we got the bow."

"And brought home a new friend," Avery said, sounding slightly less frantic.

"I wouldn't say that exactly," Saoirse said, closing the distance between us and holding out the bow. "But I am willing to try." She made a 'take it' gesture with the bow. "I believe this now belongs to you."

I hesitated to take the weapon. It was Seelie made and just because we'd managed to take it from behind enemy lines didn't mean its true purpose wasn't still in play. My fingers tingled at the sense memory of trying to touch it only a day ago. She made another gesture and this time the dark gems along the bow glittered. Maybe it was a trick of the light, but I could almost feel it calling out to me. I tightened my right hand into a fist for a count of five before taking the bow.

It didn't try to kill me or start sucking all of the magic from my body. It hummed with power, but the magic wanted to lend itself to my aid. It was the same feeling I'd gotten when Avery handed over the pendant and Rory gave me the shield. I watched as the obsidian turned almost liquid and pooled in my left palm before resolidifying into a solid hunk of rock. What was I supposed to do with this, now?

An image I hadn't thought about in months flashed through my head; me leading a cadre of women with Excalibur raised in one hand, sunlight glinting off what appeared to be armor of some kind, dotted with multi-colored stones. Maybe it was about time we started to make that a reality. I had a feeling a little dragon magic might go a long way toward making it just as formidable as the blade they'd forged for my ancestors eight hundred years ago.

"You go on a quest without me and come back with new toys. Should I be jealous?" Jules' voice came from my left and I nearly dropped both the stone and bow in my surprise.

Pocketing it, I laid the bow down on the end of the bed Rory occupied—still being tended to by medical staff—I whirled to find Jules sitting up in bed, looking much more herself. Tears welled in my eyes, blurring my vision as I threw myself at her. "You're awake! Are you okay?"

"I still feel like I got run over by a lorry, but yeah, I'm on the mend."

I felt her wince under my weight, and I eased off on my bear hug. "Don't you ever scare me like that again," I chided. "I can't afford to lose you."

"Seems like you've got plenty of candidates to fill the best friend mantle, if need be," she whispered.

"Never. There's only one you, Jules. You're irreplaceable."

"Well, that does make a girl feel special." She craned her neck. "Who is this?"

"Yes, you should introduce your new acquaintance." Emerys' voice caught me off guard from the doorway. I sat up to see her and my mother standing there waiting. I thought I spotted Gethin behind them, trying to get a glimpse of Rory.

"This is Saoirse. Nim's daughter," I said, unsure of what else to say. At the time, I'd taken it as a win that she hadn't turned us in and agreed to help us take the bow from Uther. I understood why she harbored animosity towards me. I could even see it from her perspective. After all, I felt cheated out of a life with my mother by Arthur.

"I never knew she had a child." My mother moved past Emerys into the infirmary proper and took a tentative step towards Saoirse. "I am so very sorry you lost your mother."

"Yeah, well I suppose you didn't have much say in the matter."

"No, she did not. She, too, was robbed of the opportunity to see her own flesh and blood grow and thrive," Emerys interjected. She turned to address me. "I take it that your journey led you not only to the bow, but to a piece of your past you were not yet aware of."

She was probably right. I couldn't deny that each of these quests provided me not only with some magical objects to help our fight and defend Camelot, but the people I would need to do it. And the fact that I had Aunt Nim's actual blood, her daughter willing to consider joining me made it feel almost like she wasn't gone after all. I knew it would take time for Saoirse to find her place here and for everyone to accept her, but I was ready to be patient and welcome her with open arms.

"I know you must be exhausted from everything

you've been through. Come, let's get you something to eat and a place to rest," my mother said, wrapping a gentle arm around the young Seelie woman's shoulders.

Saoirse visibly relaxed in my mother's embrace as they left the infirmary behind. With the lull in activity, the doctor who'd been fretting over Rory took the opportunity to shoo the rest of us from the space, insisting he needed to focus on healing her wound. But I didn't want to leave. I needed assurance that Rory would be okay, and I'd just gotten Jules back.

Jules seemed to sense my apprehension and climbed out from beneath the blankets. "Morgan, let's go for a walk. I could do with some exercise and some fresh air."

She looped her arm through mine and practically dragged me from the room. We stopped at my chambers long enough to grab coats and wound our way to the front entryway of the castle. I leaned against the door and watched as my breath plumed in the chilly air.

"So, do they know why you were so ill?"

"The doctors were stumped. I wasn't really with it for a lot of the time while you were away, but I do know they kept trying different things. Finally, something clicked. I woke up and the wounds stopped reopening."

"I am glad you are okay, Jules. I meant it earlier, you're irreplaceable."

"I appreciate that. I think you're pretty irreplaceable, too. But it is a good thing you're expanding your circle, gathering your allies."

"You sure you're up for sharing me?"

"I wouldn't be a very good friend if I couldn't let you flourish."

I wrapped an arm around her shoulders and pulled her close. "I really am lucky."

"So, pretty mental finding your Aunt Nim's daughter in all of this. She never even told us she had one."

I let out a breath. "I know. But I think Aunt Nim wanted to leave that part of the past behind her. If she didn't talk about Saoirse, she wouldn't have had to constantly relive the pain of losing her."

"Still, you could have grown up with a sister this whole time."

"I did. In a way. You're the closest thing to family I had, besides Nim."

"Do you think she's going to stick around?"

"Uther lied to her and was responsible for pretty much every bad thing in her life. I know she's still mad at Nim for choosing me over her, but I have to believe she'll come around. She's a good person, a lot like her mum. She's the best of them and I think we're incredibly lucky to have her on our side. Besides, Uther made her the key to retrieving the bow when he spelled it with her blood."

"He probably assumed no one would look for or notice a servant girl."

"Well, that's the thing about self-fulfilling prophecies and arrogant pricks. They always think they're smarter than the universe, and it comes back around to bite them in arse."

Jules shivered beneath my arm, and I pivoted to nudge the door back open. "Come on, let's get you inside. You're starting to get cold."

"Do you think you could convince them to let me recover in my own bed? I'm so tired of the sterile white and the constant prodding."

"I think I can manage something like that."

I'd just ushered her inside when the sound of wings beating against the air caught my attention. I turned to see a familiar form landing in the court-yard, and a second figure in its talons. Talia straightened and approached me, throwing her arms around my neck before saying a word.

"Uh, thanks?"

"Taron told me someone had been injured and I just wanted to make sure we hadn't lost our newest ally."

"We're all right. Rory's being tended to as we speak."

I watched as Taron remained in his shifted form, his breath coming out in thick puffs of smoke in the cold air. Talia caught me looking. "He won't admit it, but he's exhausted and needs to rest. But when he saw I was worried about you, he insisted we come."

"I appreciate you both checking up on me. I hope we didn't cause a diplomatic incident between the Dragons and the Seelie."

"Uther may be a power-hungry bastard, but he's not stupid enough to take us on."

I brushed a few strands of hair off my neck and realized for the first time that somewhere along the way the pendant she'd given me to conceal my identity had disappeared. I had lost it in the fray after I'd revealed myself to Arthur. "Oh, fuck. The pendant."

"It's outlived its usefulness. If someone finds it, then they've got a pretty trinket. Nothing more. I am glad to know it worked, though."

"You really came through for us." The image of the armor flashed through my head again. I moved past her to approach Taron. "You better go home and get some rest." I pressed my left hand to his snout and felt the gentle shift and motion of his head bobbing up and down. "And when you've gotten a proper night's rest, or three, I'm going to need those welding skills of yours. Something tells me you're meant to forge something else to help win this coming war." His head bobbed more forcefully this time, and I could see the expression in his eyes change, brightening with excitement. I laughed as he blew out another smoke cloud and tried to nuzzle my cheek.

Kissing the rough scales on his nose, I stepped back to allow Talia to resume her position in her brother's talons before they took to the sky again. This quest had an incredibly close call and somehow, we'd managed to escape the worst of it. We'd achieved our objective in more ways than one, but I knew we wouldn't always be this lucky. There was every possibility the next quest would land us somewhere we couldn't escape. Still, I chose to focus on the positive. My friends were safe. I was home where I belonged, and I'd managed to expand my circle of knights. For now, I would take the win. I retreated inside and wandered down to the kitchen where I found Gethin elbow-deep in decorating a cake. The moment he saw me, he relaxed. I gave him an unceremonious hug, buttercream icing smearing on both of us. It all felt incredibly normal and magical at the same time. Just what I needed. The distant whispers of what might be coming on the horizon faded. They were tomorrow's problem.

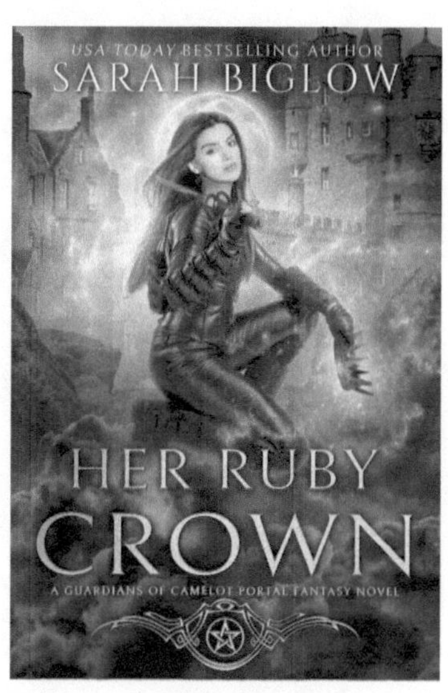

Heavy is the head that seeks the crown...

Life in Camelot has finally settled into something resembling normalcy. Morgan and her growing sisterhood of witch knights have settled into a comfortable comradery. But when a girl's night out ends with a cryptic vision, Morgan knows a new quest is upon her.

Joined by Julayne and Saoirse, she must brave the frozen forests of the Unseelie realm. A kingdom cut off from the rest of Albion, they find themselves ill-prepared for the dangers that lurk there. Their hunt for a mysterious ruby crown leads them into a tangled web of noble intrigue and violence.

Even if Morgan and her friends can find allies amongst the wilderness, it may not be enough to complete their mission and return home. Will this be the quest that finally robs Camelot of its future Queen?

Scan the QR code to get your copy of Her Ruby Crown.

ABOUT THE AUTHOR

Sarah Biglow is a *USA Today* bestselling author. She lives in Massachusetts with her husband and son. She is a licensed attorney and spends her days combatting employment discrimination as an Investigator with the Massachusetts Commission Against Discrimination.

You can find an up-to-date list of all my books here